Blue Ring Assassins

Book Three

By
Stephen Cohen

Although this book is a work of fiction, it is entwined with true historical events, facts and names.

With the exception of historical figures, all characters in this book are fictitious and any resemblance to actual persons, living or dead, is purely coincidental.
References to real places, people, events etc are only included to provide a sense of authenticity and use has been for dramatic purpose rather than historical fact.

The Blue Ring Assassins 1944-1945
ISBN

Table of Contents

Acknowledgements
Special thanks go to: -

Kelly-Mae Matt – For your help and guidance, editing and patients, which was pushed to limits at times. Thank you, forever grateful, Kelly.

Keith – Your continued help and guidance is greatly appreciated. Cover recommendation and Editing. Thank you, Keith – Badman Publishing.

Kimy – Without Kimy, the new covers would be lacking a vital element. Thank you, eagle eyed, Kimy.

Background Authentic Facts

Operation Deadheads
Polish Home Army

The operational objective was for a series of assassinations of top Nazi-ranking officers and officials in occupied Poland and was run by the Polish resistance during WWII.

The operations code name was taken from the insignia on Nazi German SS uniforms and headgear, *Totenkopf* (" Death's Head").

'Operation Heads' was a direct response by the Polish resistance Home Army due to the continued indiscriminate murders, kidnappings and torture of non-Jewish civilians in Poland by the Nazis. Between 1942 - 1944 there were thousands murdered. It is estimated that there was a minimum of 400 daily victims; 37,000 were killed at Pawiak prison alone, which was run by some very extreme, cruel Nazi officers and officials. By the end of the war, it is estimated that the Polish Home Army had somewhere between 300,000 to 600,000 members, making it one of the largest resistance groups in Europe.

Operation Bürkl – Polish Home Army

Franz Bürkl was an SS-Oberscharführer, member of the Gestapo , and commandant of Pawiak prison. He was killed on September 7th, 1943.

Stephan Klein – SS-Scharführer member of Pawiak prison administration. He was killed in 1943

Ernst Weffels was an SS-Sturmmann member of Nazi personnel of Pawiak prison. He was executed on October 1st, 1943, for cruelty and executions in the Women's Prison in Pawiak, He was known for his sadism and cruel treatment of prisoners. Weffels worked closely in cooperation with Sabina Bykowska Weffels lover and Nazi co-operator, she helped him identify Polish underground/resistance personnel.

Any Nazi officer or co-operator could and would go on the resistance list, in fact, anyone who directly or indirectly harmed any nonmilitary people would become a target. German administration, police, SS, SA, labour office and Gestapo agents. Because of the brutality of the police, the Home Army killed 361 gendarmes in 1943, and in 1944 another 584. From August to December 1942, the Home Army carried out 87 attacks on the German administration and members of the occupation forces. In 1943 this number grew radically. During the first four months of 1943, the Home Army increased these attacks to 514

Pawiak Prison – Warsaw- Poland

Pawiak Prison became a German *Gestapo* prison, then part of the Nazi concentration – death-camp system. Approximately 100,000 men and 200,000 women passed through the prison, mostly Home Army members, political prisoners, and civilians were taken hostage in street round-ups.

Operation Greif

Otto Skorzeny was an Austrian SS-*Standartenführer* (colonel) in the German Waffen-SS and became one of Hitler's favourite colonels after operation " Gran Sasso" in September 1943, which resulted in the rescue of Hitler's axis friend, Italian dictator Benito Mussolini.

Following his return to Germany, Skorzeny was summoned to meet Hitler at his headquarters at Rastenburg in East Prussia on 22 October 1944. Hitler congratulated Skorzeny and then talked with him about "Operation Greif" involving repatriating English-speaking German nationals from the USA, fully training them as German commandos and sending them behind enemy lines in France.

Dressed in US Army uniforms (the highest US Army rank used was that of colonel), armed with US Army weapons, and using US Army jeeps, the commandos were given three missions:

1. Demolition squads of five or six men were to destroy bridges, ammunition dumps, and fuel stores.
2. Reconnaissance patrols of three or four men were to reconnoitre on both sides of the Meuse River and pass on bogus orders to any US units they met, reverse road signs, remove minefield warnings, and cordon off roads with warnings of non-existent mines.
3. "Lead" commando units would work closely with the attacking units to disrupt the US chain of command by destroying field telephone wires and radio stations and issuing false orders.

Operation remorse

This British operation was run by the SOE in Hong Kong and China, which involved counterfeiting currency and smuggling. This generated over 77 million in profits for the SOE.

Herman Göring

Obersalzerg was the mountain retreat area in Bavaria, Germany where Adolf Hitler and some of the high-ranking officers like Herman Goering had residences.

Goering's residence was where he kept and displayed all his stolen or purchased art. As did Hitler.

By 26 April 1945, the complex at Obersalzberg was under attack by the Allies, so Göring moved to his castle at Mauterndorf.

Goering made his way to the US lines in hopes of surrendering to them rather than to the Soviets. He was taken into custody near Radstadt on 6 May 1945 by elements of the 36th Infantry Division of the US Army.

Goering made an appeal asking to be shot as a soldier instead of hanged as a common criminal, but the court refused. He committed suicide with a potassium cyanide capsule the night before he was to be hanged.

Mussolini

Italian Partisans capture Mussolini near Dongo village, off the shores of Lake Como on 27th April 1945, the very next day he and his then mistress are both shot.

Operation Jedburgh
The SOE and OSS

Prior to D-Day and in support of the Allied invasion of France, both agencies sent in uniformed military men and other personnel to support Operation Overlord.

Their task was to coordinate with the French resistance and cause as much disruption as possible, cutting phone lines, and delaying axis troop and vehicle movements. One of the major delays they caused was to the 2nd SS Panzer Division.

Watch out for other historical events and facts throughout the book.

Chapter One

Hannah

It's now been almost a week and Heidi has still not woken up. The doctors tell us that it's what the body does to heal itself after major trauma.

Auntie hasn't slept much, and we hear her crying every night. She has hardly left her room or eaten in days - she is distraught and we are now truly concerned about her. She is of old age after all and something like this can take a great toll on a person.

Everyone is rallying around though. We take it in turns to visit both Daphne, who is now at home convalescing, and Heidi, ensuring she is comfortable.

We have asked London for a few weeks off, but they declined, stating that the war will not wait for injured personnel. Mila has taken up the mantle and temporarily performing Heidi's duties. Petra, I think she is about to explode, her anger and hatred for the Nazi's is so deep, so we try to avoid her as much as possible. Those closest to her understand she doesn't mean to be like this, especially with us, but Petra doesn't know any other way to express her emotions.

Last night on my way to bed as I passed Heidi's room, Petra was sat on her bed reading from her poetry book. Apparently, Heidi had written a poem about Petra:

*The mirror has long stopped reflecting self.
Instead, the person I see is just a shell
void of love, consumed by hatred.
Many people miss loved ones...*

*Me...I miss myself; the old me, before being
turned into this...monster thirsting for vengeance.
My eyes open a window to a soul that pretends
strength on the outside but cries for help within me.*

*I might have escaped death, but I remain trapped by
the past that moulded me.*

The world is cruel to a woman's heart.

*War has stained the earth with blood, but no cries are
heard
for those abused by the hands of narcissistic men.
Nights still haunt me with images of torture and
molestation.*

*Memories bombard me as I remain stagnant before
the mirror,
lost in gaze at the person staring right back at
me...and she smiles.*

*not happily, but with insanity. Her soul is lost to the
dark sides of war,
but finds purpose in bringing retribution to those
responsible
for what she's become...*

It certainly is a true reflection of Petra, but then it could also be about any woman who has suffered at the hands of the tyrant Adolf Hitler and his Nazi regime.

When she wasn't working, poetry was Heidi's favourite pass time. She told me once that she started writing poems at the age of 10.

'Artist' is now officially on London's missing list, presumed dead, Honestly, although I don't have feelings for the man, I miss him! but all I can think about is Heidi, so my feelings and thoughts that are lacking for him, is just how it is, right now.

The end of January 1944 is fast approaching and although our request for time off was declined officially, we had not received any mission. Until today.

Hans Frank, head of General Government, Occupied Poland now comes into our crosshairs. Naturally, we must follow orders, but none of us wanted to go in case Heidi woke up. At least she always has someone there, although not Petra or I at this time.

We are to meet the Polish resistance, the Home Army, who over the previous twelve months or so have grown in strength. They have had many successful operations over the past couple of years. Very diverse in their approach, they not only target high-ranking German officers but anyone who commits any kind of cruel act upon the local population are fair game to this group.

General Stefan Rowenki, Head of the Home Army planned and executed a three-stage uprising against the Nazis last year. Though he was not aware at the time, he was laying the groundwork for a joint operation with the Russian Army which is now underway. The Red Army are fast approaching from the east, we know this from the papers constantly reporting on the allied success. It is certain that the Red Army will become the liberators of Poland.

All across Poland the Home Army are having success after success. Yes, they are experiencing heavy losses but their determination and resilience shines through.

According to our brief, the Home Army have now joined forces with the Red Army and Operation Tempest is well underway. In an effort to aid in the successful downfall of the Wehrmacht in Poland, we have been tasked with assassinating Hans Frank. This kind of commitment to the downfall of the Nazi regime is something we admire greatly.

Another resistance group in Poland, the Polish Secret State, who are loyal to the now exiled (Republic Polish Government) in London have requested help in this attempt. They have obtained information about a special train from Kraków to Lviv on the 29th – 30th of January 1944 which will be carrying Frank.

Petra and I head for Poland, however not without reservations about leaving Heidi in her current situation. When she comes round, she should have all her family with her. Besides that, Petra and I have many questions about the man who shot them.

On this occasion I didn't take my sketchbook, I didn't feel like sketching. We sat mostly in silence throughout the whole journey. Concern for Heidi is at the forefront of my mind, and I am sure that Petra feels the same. We need to complete this mission and return home as quickly as possible.

We parachute into our drop zone and are awaiting contacts. Having hidden our chute we head for a remote farm building just a mile away from our target train line.

For the actual operation, not knowing the exact time, it was decided that the best way to tackle this was a well-placed plunger charge on the line and not a timed device, which will cause the train to derail. Then we come out shooting everything that moves as they attempt to escape. For this we will need about thirty resistance fighters, hidden on either side of the tracks with a good line of fire.

One thing in our favour was that the resistance has a man at the departure station. So, we will at least know when it has left. Other factors then come into play: train speed and if it makes any other stops along its route.

The device is prepared and the plunger tested to our satisfaction. The team is assembled and we all head off to the objective. Upon arrival we send someone off to place and hide the charge on the railway track. That completes stage one. Now, all we need to do is wait for the man at the station to make contact.

Having several hours to wait we take the time to do some reconnaissance of the surrounding area. Small teams head off in different directions and are given an hour to report back. The local resistance knows the area well and with this in mind it's decided that their leader should plan our escape route and contingency plan.

Having been informed when the train had left, we calculate that zero hour is fast approaching, so we head off and take up our positions. About an hour later we saw the train coming our way and I prepare the plunger, connecting to the battery. Everyone is well back to ensure they don't get tangled in the wreckage.

The ground is now trembling beneath us as the train gets ever closer. With the train over the charge, I push down on the plunger, and almost immediately there was a loud explosion. Then came the sounds of metal twisting and colliding as the rail cars came off the tracks and dug into the ground. Large clouds of steam and hissing come from the engine as it spills to rest on its side. The explosive wave hit us first, which was occupied with the feeling of stone and grit digging into my body.

The smell of coal and heated steam filling the air, I take a quick look around to make sure everyone is ok. Those that I can see are standing but it would seem, like myself, they haven't yet noticed they are suffering some injuries from the flying debris. Adrenaline has taken over for the time being!

We hadn't taken that factor into consideration, flying grit and stone caused some of us injuries.

Derailed, the train comes to a mangled stop. A whistle sounds, our agreed signal, and everyone moves forward at the ready. The shooting starts with the first steps taken. We all move forward towards the mangled wreckage; rail cars are laid on their sides on both sides of the tracks. Some have even come to a stop on top of others. Between the short bursts of gunfire, you can hear the cries of those still trapped in the wreckage, cries that wouldn't be heard for much longer.

Without warning, there is an even louder explosion, which came from the front of the wreckage. As if rehearsed, we all turned simultaneously to watch the engine burst open in a blaze of smoke and flying metal. Something else we hadn't factored in; it was by luck alone, that none of our comrades were near there.

It's all over within a short time, you could hear the periodic single shot as some of the passengers were finished off. We enter the carriages to check everyone is dead. We had no losses and so it didn't take too long to ensure everyone on the train was taken out.

We all make our escape, heading for the resistance hideout. Upon our arrival, it only then became apparent how many of us are injured. Like me, many of us have head and arm cuts and even small pieces of stone embedded in our skin. It takes a few hours but eventually we are all patched up and once the adrenaline had faded, the pain started. At least no one died.

Pleased with the speed and unmitigated dedication of the team, we head off, mission accomplished.

It took almost a full day to get home and our first thought was to get an update regarding Heidi. However, there was a message waiting for us from London.

Mission unsuccessful, report to London immediately for debrief. Plane standing by.
Message ends.

We had never been summoned to London before, this was a little concerning. Petra refuses to go, which maybe is a good idea. The last thing we need right now is her particular colourful approach. I suggest she stays at home and that I take this trip alone.

Before heading off to the plane, I call in at the hospital to check on Heidi. Auntie was at her bedside when I arrived.

"Any change auntie?" I inquire.

"Oh, my dear what has happened to you?" she asks, referring to all the minor cuts on my hands and face.

"Please don't concern yourself auntie, they are nothing. How is Heidi?" I repeat.

"There is no change, Hannah. Come let's get a nurse to clean you up," she insists as she asks one of the nurses for help.

About twenty minutes later and after the nurse had completed her duties with me, I was on my way to the waiting plane and what I was guessing not going to be a very nice reception.

I went over the mission in my head during the flight over, how could we have missed him? I kept asking myself. We checked everyone, inside and outside of every carriage. I was sure of it.

The plane landed and as we came to a stop, a car approached the plane. A female driver, dressed in army uniform, got out of the driver's seat and walked round to open the door for me. Umm, I thought, these Brits are very well mannered.

As we drove into the city, I got my first glimpse of the destruction Hitler has and continues to rain down on the British. Buildings reduced to nothing but piles of rubble and wood line the streets with the residents searching through it for their lost possessions.

Just as in other countries, some have lost everything they owned. Young and old couples just sat on their broken homes, grief-stricken, whilst consoling each other the best they can.

Despite all the destruction and loss, the majority it seems, are going about their daily business. Everyone including the children are carrying these strange little boxes, over their shoulders, some held to their bodies by string while others have straps.

"What is that everyone is carrying?" I ask the driver.

"Gas masks, miss. We have to carry them everywhere with us in case of chemical bombs," she replies.

"Is that a real threat?"

"The top brass seems to think so yes," she says.

Minutes later we arrive at our destination.

"Here we are, miss. Baker Street. The general is waiting for you. This way," she says with an extended arm.

I was trying to take in as much as I could, I am in the headquarters of the British SOE after all.

We pass many rooms, doors mostly closed but you could hear the activity behind them was intense. The corridor was a hive of activity too, people rushing in and out of different rooms. Organised chaos would be the best way to describe it.

We arrive at a closed-door and she doesn't knock, instead she walks in, and I follow. The room is lined with chairs around the walls with all manner of people sitting and waiting their turn. It reminded me of a doctor's waiting room, no one was talking, simply sitting in complete silence.

"Take a seat, miss. I will let them know you're here," she instructs me as she walks towards another door, on which she knocks and walks in, closing it firmly behind her.

I am sitting here for well over an hour, watching people coming and going constantly. Some simply walk straight into the next room, while others like me wait to be called through by a nicely dressed older woman.

Again and again, a steady stream of people come and go; it was the busiest office I have ever been in. At last it was my turn.

"Come this way, please," the lady gestures with a stretched arm.

I follow her through the closed door only to enter another room, one with a single desk and two chairs.

"Please take a seat. The General will be with you in just a moment," she says and takes her seat behind her desk.

This was a strange thing; I have left one waiting room just to be sat in another. Within minutes the other door opened and a well-dressed uniformed fellow, with files tucked under his arm, beckons me in.

"General. The lady you have been expecting," he says as I walk into the room.

"Thank you, that will be all. Close the door on your way out," from a tall man with a moustache and receding hairline.

"Sir, I ..." but I am stopped mid-sentence by him with one finger raised in the air.

"Good morning, Hannah. Please sit. Would you like some tea?" he asks

"I prefer coffee, sir, if you have it. Black no sugar," I request as I take a seat.

He walks over to a table and starts making the drinks, whilst doing so, he continues talking. "Quite the mess you have left over in Poland. Walk me through it, please."

While he makes the beverages, I provide him with a full breakdown of the operation. He listens intensely without interruption, even as he places my coffee on his desk in from me.

"You ladies over the past few years have never missed a target as far as I am aware. Correct?" he enquires as he lights a cigarette.

He learns forward and offers me the lit cigarette. What a quaint custom, I thought to myself as I took it.

"Mission wise, we have missed two targets. The one you pulled us off from in Albania and the last one." I take a small drag of my cigarette and continue. "Honestly, though I don't know how we missed the last one. We shot everyone, inside and outside of the carriages. There was no way he could have survived, sir," I replied as I take a puff of my cigarette.

"We had to pull you off the Albanian Assassination as we had heard he had a plan for escape. We don't actually shoot our people for no reason, Hannah," he remarks, before continuing. "It would seem he jumped from the train; he must have been standing between the carriages while the train was derailing. Pure speculation you understand but very plausible," he stands up and starts walking around.

There were a few seconds of silence apart from him tapping his hands together behind his back. Quite annoying really. As he stands looking out the window he asks " How is Heidi doing?"

"Currently still in a coma. The doctors say she will hopefully come out of it," I reply.

"Ghastly business. I understand that it's a hard time for you all, but you must stay completely focused on the task at hand, Hannah," he remarks.

I simply acknowledge him with a slight nod of my head. He continues.

"Regarding the matter of your side-line activities. My predecessor and Falcon allowed this to continue, but I have to say I'm not at all happy with it," he says, attitude lacing his tone.

"But sir, we..." He stops me mid-sentence. "Hannah, you work for the British government and as such you will conduct yourselves in an appropriate manner, at all times. Do I make myself clear?" slamming his hand down on his desk and glaring at me with stone cold eyes.

Good job Petra isn't here, she would have told him to "Fuck Off".

"Yes, sir." I had no intention of complying, but I agreed just to keep the peace. Besides, we will never rest until we have found and killed the man who attacked our girls.

Pulling his lips back into his mouth and shaking his head he leaned forward and picked up another cigarette, lit it and continued. I do believe he is upset with me; he didn't offer me one this time.

"Now I have to talk to you about a very delicate matter. This is highly classified and is only to be talked about with those on this list," he says as he hands me a piece of paper from his desk.

"You are aware that Falcon and Viper are currently working in Asia as part of our Force 136 team. Yes?"

"Yes, sir."

"We have an ongoing highly secret operation in Hong Kong. I need you to train a team of ladies in, let's say, some of your more colourful skills," He requests.

"Sorry, sir. I am not with you?" I state, confused.

Surely, he isn't talking about our, now how did he put it, *side-line activities*. Just moments ago, he had finished telling me that we can't do that anymore. Talk about dual standards.

"Sir. You will have to be clearer!" I state.

"You ladies are very skilled at smuggling items out of a country. We know this, because of all your ill-gotten gains you send to America," he remarks with confidence.

These people know everything, Falcon must have produced detailed reports on us.

"Just to be clear, you want us to train your ladies to smuggle items out of Hong Kong?" I inquire.

"Yes," he simply replies.

This is a turn up for the books, now we are training the British in highly illegal activities!

"Ummm, firstly, we already have our own ladies that can perform this without any further training. Secondly, if we do this then as we are breaking the law, we will expect to be paid," I propose.

"Paid? We are already paying you all as agents," he replies angrily.

"That's for our duties as active agents, not for performing duties outside of that remit." I take a sip of my coffee and continue. "We can do this, but we will want 5% of everything we bring in," I replied, without even knowing what it is he wants us to smuggle, or do, at this point.

He sits and starts tapping his lower lip, pondering my proposal. After a short period, he gets up out of his chair and walks around to stand in front of his desk. At this point, I couldn't help the thought that I was about to be arrested or worse. He stares into my eyes, offers his hand out to me and replies.

"Ok. Use your own ladies and we will give you 5% of everything you deliver to us. Get them ready and will we organise their transport to Hong Kong."
We shake hands, and he gestures towards the door.

I can't believe what has just happened, I am bewildered beyond belief! I need a drink and a smoke.

The receptionist asks if I need the car to return me to the airport and I accept. On route, I ask the driver if there is a café, we can make a quick stop at.

" Café, miss? Do You want a cup of tea?" she enquires.

"No, I need a drink, something much stronger than tea," I reply.

"Then you will require a bar, miss. Here cafés are for tea and cake, a bar is where we go for a stiff one," she tells me.

I am learning a lot about the British customs today. Their mannerisms, culture, I have even experienced first-hand their stiff upper lip.

"Then let's stop for a strong drink. The pilot can wait for me," I state eagerly.

"Sorry, miss. I can't drink on duty, but I will come in and have a soft drink with you certainly," she replies.

British culture is full of strange customs. It is my first time visiting, but I feel I must return one day and learn more about this strong-willed country.

We have an hour in a typical English bar which was full of Service personnel and the general population, all interacting together as if there was no war going on. Over in Europe, the cafés usually have several German soldiers in them, and everyone needs to be so careful what they talk about. Say the wrong thing and someone hears, you can be shot on the spot.

Some of the gentlemen are playing a game so I ask my driver to tell me about it.

"That is called darts, miss, it's in most pubs," she tells me.

"And the one with a picture of Hitler on it with so many holes punctured in it from the darts, you can only just make it out," I ask her.

"Oh, that's just a bit fun, miss," she replies.

It made me break a little smile, life without tyranny is so different here. Even in Switzerland, you have to be careful due to all the spies, you never know who you're talking to.

It was time to head for my plane, return home and inform the girls of the current situation and forthcoming mission.

Chapter Two

Hannah

Petra met me at the plane, and we head straight to the hospital to visit Heidi. She tells me there hasn't been any change since I left.

I give her the full rundown on my visit to London. She agrees with me regarding the General's instruction to stop our other activities. Her exact words were:

"FUCK THAT!"

We discuss the best options for the Hong Kong mission, and decide it is better for us to stay close by Heidi.   Besides, Daphne is our top person for the smuggling aspect of our operation and therefore the best person to send. We just have to talk her into it. She normally has nothing to do with entering any war-torn theatre and might be apprehensive. We need Mila to continue filling in for Heidi and Christa is busy with the dog training, so it will have to be one of the sisters or maybe even both of them, who will go with Daphne to Hong Kong. It will be a solid first field assignment for them both, and with Daphne guiding them, we won't have to worry.

It would have been nice to see Falcon and Viper again, but one thing Petra and I now know, is that our minds aren't totally committed to anything else but Heidi. Arriving at the hospital we head for Heidi's ward. As we approach, we see every one of our ladies hugging and crying on each other. They all surround auntie in a group effort to console her. Not only did this stop both of us in our tracks, but we also simultaneously grab each other and stare intensely into each other's eyes. Even the normally emotionless, cold Petra couldn't hold back the overwhelming feelings of loss as the realisation that we have lost Heidi floods in. We speak no words; we just hold each other as the tears flood down our faces.

We join the others and together, we mourn the loss of one of the most dedicated, loving, caring friends we are ever likely to meet. One by one we visit her for the last time. The room is as empty as my heart, the pain in my stomach is almost preventing me from breathing. She lays motionless on a cold metal table, covered by a white sheet. The air is full of her perfume, the scent of summer flowers overpowering the lingering stench of death. She is wearing her favourite lipstick. I am guessing we have auntie to thank for that. I reminisce with her for a few moments, recalling some of our greatest times whilst holding her cold, lifeless hand. I lean in and kiss her on her forehead for a final time and make one last declaration to her.

" From this moment forward, I will not rest until the person that did this to you has suffered like no other. This I promise on the pain of death."

I run my other hand over her cheek and then gently place her hand back beside her body. As I come to the open door, I turn and look at Heidi, one last time. The passing of a loved one is something that most people will have to endure during wartime, some more than once. It doesn't get easier though.

Over the next couple of days or so we hardly speak to each other, simply working through the grief in our own ways. Auntie was out most days attending to the arrangements for Heidi's final resting place. She wanted to return Heidi to Austria, so she could lay with her parents. The logistics of that at this time proved to be too complicated. Instead, Heidi will be laid to rest in the local cemetery close by. It takes place tomorrow.

The sisters have been spending the past few days at Daphne's house, a little extra training prior to their trip. We are waiting on a message from London informing us that their papers are ready, and transport is arranged. London has however found it in their souls to give us a few days to bury our friend. This was unexpected.

Mila and Petra are also out for most of the day, attempting to find any witnesses from the shooting in an effort to obtain a description of the man. We also have someone in the airport that has agreed to provide us with the passenger list from Daphne's flight.

We think it's the same man Daphne told us about that was watching them at the bank in Argentina. This means he travelled on that flight and therefore used a name. Now, it most certainly will be a false one, but it's a start. The other thing to take into consideration is that people that use false names usually use the same ones, which will make it easier to track him. The more background information we have, the sooner we will come face to face with him.

It's not like Petra to take such an interest in this kind of work, she is normally a hands-on kinda girl, "turn up and kill them" person. One thing about her though, once committed to a task, she will see it through. Mila is hard at work, using every resource she has to track this man down. Others are dotted around the house, some alone, sitting in reflection, others gathered around the kitchen table. As for Petra, I have found her a couple of times in our piano room, just either looking out the window or sitting at the piano.

I asked her yesterday what she was doing in there, as we don't usually use that room. The piano, a beautiful black grand dominates the space - sitting in front of the large window, the outside scenery reflecting off its well-polished surface, it stands alone in the unfurnished room.

"It's peaceful in here and there aren't any reminders of Heidi," she replies.

We are all aware that Petra has only one emotion, anger, but over the past few days, she has been showing a softer more compassionate side. Placing a single hand on my shoulder as she walks past me at the kitchen table. Sitting with auntie, holding her hand. I do find this a little unnerving.

Auntie has taken to sleeping in Heidi's room, she tells me it makes her feel close to her. I wanted to suggest we cover everything and lock the door, never to be used again, in her memory. But if it helps auntie through her grieving, then so be it.

The day of Heidi's funeral has arrived. It's an emotional day for us all. We make our way to the church, not one of us with dry eyes. The clonking of shoes on the pavement, the birds chirping in the trees drowned out by the sounds of many girls sobbing. Girls linked together, arm in arm, hand in hand, as we walk in two lines, totally in unison. It must have looked like one of those death marches.

Upon our arrival, the priest was already on station at the grave site. His words, although pleasant enough, didn't really resonate with most of us. We are not known for our Godly ways. As he came to the end, auntie stepped forward - she had brought one of Heidi's poems and recited it for us.

Do not grieve my passing,
memories everlasting.
Do not weep for me,
for in your heart, I rest.
Steady your trembling
heart and hands, give comfort to those
in greater need.
Do not seek out the darkness
and company of gathering dust to weep.
Rejoice in my life for I have only returned
from whence I came.

Some of the most moving words we have ever heard. Fresh tears rolling down everyone's face as we hang on every word. For me, they brought a little calmness to my trembling, pain-stricken heart and to the gathering hatred in my mind, towards the man who took her. It's as if she knew one day that one of us would be taken. It's war and in these times of constant threat to life, it's inevitable that one or more of us would meet our end. More so for us than the everyday person I guess, due to our activities.

One saving grace is that we live in Switzerland. If this had happened in an occupied country then this simple ceremony might not even have taken place. And if it had, then it would not have been as it was. Scattered across these countries are graves, marked or unmarked, in most cases, where the fallen lay was where they are buried.

We head for home and gather in the kitchen, except Petra, whom we thought had gone to her room. Moments later the house fills with the sound of the piano. I asked auntie if she had hired a pianist for the day. It had never crossed her mind. We all head for the piano room and to our amazement, it was Petra playing. Beethoven's 'Moonlight Sonata', a very touching, moving piece of music.

I for one had no idea she could play an instrument, let alone such an emotional piece like this. Watching her play was like nothing I had ever seen before. You could feel the emotion through each and every note as she played. Her facial expressions merely extenuated the emotions. Her fingers, gliding across the keys, then at certain points seem to halt as if set in stone, as she energised the notes. The swaying of her body as she moved up and down the keys, her eyes, constantly closed, but tightening as she feels her way through the piece. The corner of her mouth would rise up, not in a smile, but in a thoughtful manner as the notes resonated through her. I look around the room to see if I was the only one with tears running down my cheek. I was not alone, there wasn't a dry eye in the room. It became clear to me now why she spent so much time in this room over the past few days.

When she had finished, she paused for a moment, closed the lid, took a deep breath and composed herself. As she walked past us, we didn't speak to her, we just wiped the tears from our eyes and nodded at her in adulation. She stopped at door and turned around and stated: "That's enough of that, now let's go get that fucking bastard!"

Grief is a process, and we all go through it differently, Petra has reached the 'anger' stage, I guess.

We were about to find out she wasn't the only one. From nowhere, auntie releases a flood of pent-up emotion. Jumping up from her chair at the table, throwing her mug across the room, she unleashes on us all.

"She would still be here if it wasn't for you people, you're the reason she is dead," with a look of disgust in her eyes, her redden cheeks highlight the angry tears as they flow.

"We all love you, auntie, you're like a mother to us all, you're upset and it's understandable," Daphne interrupts with disbelief in her voice.

"Death follows you everywhere you go and now you have taken the only person I had left in my life. My cherished Heidi!"

Auntie sits back down and places her hands over her face to hide the flood of tears. In silence, I usher the girls out of the kitchen. I advised the girls to leave her to herself, she needs time. I for one understand that she needs someone to blame for the death of our Heidi. Blaming us wasn't something I expected though. I could see that the other girls are shocked by auntie's outburst, I explain that everyone deals with grief differently and that Heidi was her only family member left in her life, the war had taken them all now.

Over the next few days if auntie wasn't in Heidi's room, then she was at her graveside. I was becoming concerned for her health, she wasn't eating much at all. Petra reckons she will come around when she is ready. I am not so sure. Every time we do see her, she hardly speaks anymore. Instead, when she does look at us, all we can find is hatred in her gaze.

It has taken London almost a week but finally, the girls' new ID's and travel papers have arrived. They are to travel at the end of February, Falcon will meet them at the airport. I was going to write him a letter but decided he might think I am going soft.

Petra and Mila have gathered as much information as they can at this time about the shooter. Each day they are meticulously going through it. Daphne has a contact who works for one of the American Intelligence agencies. She has sent the list of names to him. We can't use London for any of this now due to the strict instructions given to us.

Like London, the US have contacts all over the world. Within a few days, she has a phone call. There is a man that has just bought an island in the Caribbean. He paid cash for it, and he purchased it in one of the names from our list.

This is the best lead we have had, so Petra and I waste no time. First, we head to Washington DC to meet with Daphne's contact and collect the intel he has. We travel on our British papers as this will not cause any alarm to anyone. From the airport, we head straight into the city and our meeting place. One of the many parks in the city, it's quite a large park, dotted with trees and bench seats along the many pathways. People walking their dogs, mothers pushing prams, people sitting and reading the paper. Although we had instructions to follow to our area, we are suddenly approached by a young lad.

"Excuse me, miss. Is your name, Hannah, from Switzerland?" he inquires.

"Why yes. How may I help you?" I replied.

He hands me a large brown envelope and speaks. "With regards from your American cousin." Then, as quickly as he appeared, the lad runs away.

The Americans do like the cloak and dagger stuff that is for sure.

We sit down on a nearby bench and take a look at what is inside the envelope. There is a copy of the sales report with the name Klaus Schneider, which matches one of the names Petra and Mila had on their list. Sadly, no picture is included but there is also a map with the island clearly marked. It is approximately 100 miles off the north coast of Venezuela. Immediately, we head back to the airport, where we purchase two tickets and head for Miami. We would have liked to stay in the US and take a look around, but this wasn't a sightseeing trip. This was all about revenge for Heidi.

Once we arrive in Puerto La Cruz, South America, we find a hotel. We are very tired and need to rest up. The heat here is stifling, you break out into a sweat just walking slowly.

After we are fully rested, we go shopping for some thinner clothing and a couple of sidearms. I am surprised how easily you can buy weapons here. That sorted, we then start making enquiries about how to get to this island.

The choice is either take a boat or fly into Isla La Tortuga, then head to the most eastern side of the island. The island we are looking for is situated five miles east of there.

We opted for the plane, it's quicker and besides, our last boat trip didn't actually go too well. We are told that there is a hotel on the island which also provides boat tours, fishing trips etc.

It takes a few hours but finally arrive on Tortuga. The flight over was a quiet one. I spent the time contemplating what I am going to do, once I get to look Heidi's killer in the eyes.

As the plane began its descent, I was amazed as I looked out the window at how many small, but beautiful islands there are in this part of the world.

We settle into our hotel and act like every other tourist. It made for a great cover. Dress in light coloured clothing, knee length skirts that flow in the sea breeze. Loose fitting tops to help keep us cool in the tropical sun. We have travelled to some beautiful countries and seen some lovely sights, but this island is in a league of its own. The pure white sand and azure blue sea is something to behold, along with the warm sea breeze - this place is pure heaven.

The hotel is stunning, we have a bar right on the sand and for a moment I forgot what we are here for. Petra soon brought me back to the real world though.

"Come on, Hannah. Forget the fucking sea, you will see more than you need soon enough," she reminds me.

We charter a fishing boat for a couple of days. With a little extra money, the owner agrees to take us anywhere we would like to go.

"We are going to get really creative when we come face to face with this guy, Petra," I reminded her because we don't want to just shoot him. "He has to suffer and for a very long time."

"I don't need reminding, Hannah. I'm going rip his fucking skin off, one layer at a time," she replies.

I wasn't quite sure how she was going to do that, but it sounded right to me.

Dressed in loose attire, similar to what the local fishing women wear, hiding our weapons beneath our clothes with ease, we set off. The sea was calm, which we are pleased about.

Taking our time, we arrive on the east side of the main island, not too close to his but close enough to use our binoculars and ask questions.

"There is a lot of activity going on over there. Whose island is that?" I asked our captain.

"That's Schneider Island. It's just been bought a few weeks ago by some foreign gentleman. He is spending vast amounts of money on it too," he replied and continued. "Every three or four days he hires just about every boat he can on the island to take out more supplies he has had flown in."

"I can see there is a lot of construction going on," I remarked.

"All we know is he is very rich and pays well. It used to be two islands until he constructed the walkway to link them both," he remarks.

" Ok, captain. You can take us in now, that's about enough fishing for one day," I request.

We were too far out to make out anyone's face but there are over thirty people on that island. Mostly construction workers. Our man has to be among them though.

Overnight at our hotel Petra and I discuss our options and we decide the best way to that island is to help the fisherman on their next delivery. They all seem to like money, so it will be easy to bribe one of them without too much trouble.

We patiently wait and watch for a rush of activity and for our newfound friend to give us the sign that it is loading time. Sitting around taking in the sights, switching between sun and shade. This took three days, both Petra and I have spent far too much time in the sun, and we have burned a little. The locals are great though, they provide us with their local sunburn recipe, and it seems to work although has a strange cent.

Wearing local clothing, brightly coloured skirts and tops to blend in, we head for the quayside near the airstrip and start loading. This time we are on a much larger fishing boat and the captain is teaching me about boat handling. They have some strange names for the boat sides, stern, bow, port side, it's all very new but interesting.

After a couple of hours sitting around the boat, waiting for the captain to sort his paperwork out, we are on our way to Schneider Island. Naming the Island after yourself is a little vain I think, or maybe he just doesn't have an imagination.

Within an hour we were at his island and awaiting our turn to unload. There is only a small jetty, which could accommodate just two boats at a time. It was our turn, and when our captain ties up his boat, he asks us to help remove some of the items still waiting on the jetty to be taken up to the site.

This was our first chance to get a good look around. We grab a box each and follow the rest of the workers off the jetty and along a newly laid pathway. I could see so much activity; there are people everywhere, all going about their duties. We're carrying provision for the workforce and were instructed to take them to the workers' camp, which is situated on the other end of the island, as far away from the main house as it could possibly be. So, we now knew that the workers are staying on the island, which makes things complicated.

Still no sign of the owner though. We need to have a roam around but without drawing any suspicion. Our captain has transported mainly timber. He didn't need us to unload as he has a small crane onboard which he uses for his fishing nets. Dropping our boxes with all the other provisions close by the makeshift kitchen tent, we notice there are a couple of women walking around the site with water buckets, perfect for us to use as a cover. We grab a bucket and head off in different direction but being very aware of the lack of time we have. It will only take our captain thirty minutes to unload.

Meeting back at the boat and just in time, the captain was shouting for us to get on board as he had to move. We head to the bow of the boat for a debrief.

"I didn't see anyone but construction workers Petra. How about you?" I asked.

She was silent, her gaze seemed to penetrate right through me, as if she had something to say, but didn't know how. Or couldn't.

"I need a moment, to process what I have just seen, Hannah."

There must have been a quizzical look on my face or maybe some frustration at this, and she continued, "Oh, if I need a minute, you're going to need a week," her voice tinged with disbelief.

I could tell this was serious, she didn't once use any colourful language. But what could it be?

"Just spit it out Petra, you're worrying me now," I insisted.

"Take a deep breath and sit-down Hannah. This is going to truly hurt," she says as she takes my arm as I sit down.

We all know that Petra isn't one for dramatics, but I am now worried she is about to tell me that it's my father or something.

"I had to look three times myself, Hannah, because I couldn't belief who I was looking at. I had to be sure."

" Ok, so who did you see?"

"It's Otto! He is the one that shot Daphne and killed Heidi," she says holding my hand.

I shoot up and push her in the shoulder.

"No! No! No!, It can't be. You're mistaken," I cry out as I sit back down and place my hands over my face to cover the tears. "Let's get the hell out of here Petra, right now!"

Otto, to whom I had given my heart. 'Artist', as we believed him to be, a British agent posing as a Nazi.

Petra

Hannah is in total disbelief by the recent revelations regarding Otto. So much so that she hasn't spoken a word since.

We are making our way home as we have been away too long already. As for that 'Arschloch' (asshole), Otto, I am sure we will deal with him once Hannah has processed the situation.

The journey home was one of the worst I have ever had to endure. I have no idea what to say to Hannah, words just don't seem fitting at this time.

We have spent weeks tracking the fourth man down. Now we have found him, all I want to do is kill him. I have no option but to wait for Hannah, this has to be her call. If it was my choice, I would have shot him there and then without mercy. I am sure that Hannah will realise he has to die, it's just a matter of time.

Chapter Three

Petra

Auntie has disappeared.

We arrive home to the news a couple of days after the mission. It was Miles who found her gone after going to wake her up and finding her bed empty. I love her like she is my own mother, and although I sympathise with her, I do not agree with this change in attitude towards us all.

To make matters even more difficult, London have been asking for updates regarding 'Operation Remorse'. I am out of my depth; I don't deal with these kinds of things. So, I've asked Mila to send word that they have arrived and made contact with Falcon. I am hoping that will pacify London and provide us with some more time.

Regarding Hannah, three days have passed and she still hasn't spoken a fucking word. She storms in to every room, constantly red-faced, her eyes glazed over, and grunting if anyone speaks to her. I wouldn't want to be him, once she decides his fate. Seeing Hannah this way is un-nerving, she is normally so level-headed and controlled, it's fucking my head up. The other girls are giving her a wide berth; it's obviously scaring the hell out of them too.

Another two days pass and the radio is going crazy with traffic from Hong Kong and London. It's as if London is tracking our girls. The girls are on route back with the first shipment. I have no option but to approach Hannah and try and break her out of her silence.

She has gone on one of her walks, which means she will more than likely be in the woods somewhere. After four hours I track her down, the peaceful, calming sounds of the forest are overshadowed by someone hysterically crying. It sounds like she has completely lost control, I haven't set eyes on her yet but I can hear her breathing is sporadic, her cries are so loud, they drown out the sounds of nature around us. As I turn the corner on the path, I witness something I never want to see again. Hannah, kicking and punching the fuck out of a tree. I'll admit, this is completely fucking me up, she is so messed up by the situation with Otto.

I have no option but to approach her, or at least attempt to. Before I get too close, I shout her name out a few times. This was a defensive move, the state she is in, approaching unannounced could end with a punch to the face.

Taking one step at a time, I get within striking distance. I am totally ready to repel any move Hannah might attempt, but I can't shake the feeling that maybe it would be good for her to hit someone, to release the anger she feels inside. It would be better than hitting a tree, and maybe less painful and bloody. I can see blood dripping from her knuckles now.

I take a couple of steps closer, never having an urge to hug another woman, I am having a strong feeling it would be the right thing to do. Stretching out my arm, I pull it back, this is totally alien to me. Hannah needs this, I have to overcome my own inner feelings, I take a deep breath and whilst thinking *"Fuck it"* I place my hand on her right shoulder, kind of awkwardly though.

I could feel her body trembling, I step in closer, and possibly using a little too much power, pull her in, our bodies clunk together, like a couple of large wooden logs, neither of us feeling at ease. A few seconds go by and I feel Hannah's arms wrap around me, I could sense her apprehension. She then tightened her hug and slumped head on my shoulder, I could feel her breathing slowing down.

No words are spoken, but this felt right for the moment, regardless of how fucking uncomfortable this is making me feel, it's for my sister. After a few minutes I tell her:

" Let it all out, Hannah. It will help you to process."

Hannah disengages from the embrace and takes a step back and with a look of disbelief on her face and snarls. "Bloody process, what do you call all this? this isn't sorrow or grief Petra, it's total UNCONTROLLABLE ANGER!"

Hannah starts stomping around, the sounds of breaking twigs under her feet fill the air around us.

"What are we going to do about that then, Hannah? We are going to fucking kill him, yes?" I ask.

"No, oh no, not before we take everything he has built and loves," she replies.

Thank fuck. At least Hannah is engaging now, this is a step forward. There are a few minutes of silence, I rip some cloth from my shirt and walk towards Hannah, asking he to let me take a look at her hands. While I am wrapping her wounds she asks me,

" Why were you looking for me, Petra?"

"London wants to know where we have been over the past few days," I inform her on our way back home.

Hannah
February 1944

I instruct Mila to inform London that we have been searching for auntie and the family of Otto. Requesting any assistance, they can provide to help in tracking down his family if he has any.

The response was swift!

"Artist family: father, dead. Mother alive living in England with his wife and child. They have been informed of artists death." Message Ends.

Now that I have all the information, I require time to put my plan into action. London's objective at this time is securing their first shipment from Hong Kong and so we are being left alone. The girls are on their way back from the far east, travelling by air.

We need time to complete our own first objective, find and secure Otto's family. I instruct Mila to find his family now that London has provided us with a general location. A few days later she tracked them down in an area called Yorkshire.

We get our forger to prepare some travel documents for Petra and myself, for flying into the closest airfields near his family. We then arrange our transport.

Landing a few miles away on one of the RAF airfields, we request a car and driver using our SOE papers as authority to do so. It's amazing how easy people follow instructions once you start to flash spy documentation and identity cards around.

We have approximately five hours to get back to the plane, there is no time to waste so, I instruct the pilot to refuel and await our return.

Arriving at 'Artists' home in England, within an hour we set straight into the issue at hand. Kidnapping his family and taking them to a secure place. Doing a quick reconnaissance of our surrounding our only option is to go for a quick smash and grab, then return to the airfield by the same road.

We walk up to the house and just walk straight in, armed with handguns at the ready. We split up and gather the residents in the kitchen. The only voices you hear are ours,

"Be silent and no harm will come to you."

Surprisingly, they conform very easily to our requests. Maybe they could see, or at least get a sense, that arguing or resisting would cause them great suffering. Or simply, two young women with handguns in their home is enough. Although quiet, we could see the fear in their faces, their trembling bodies and beads of sweat forming on their faces. The women holding closely the young boy as if to protect him. Petra and I had to say very little, our determination, stern faces and vocal tones, strong body language and our weapons are enough to scare the living hell out of two females and a young boy.

We walk them out to the car, reminding them to stay silent, or they will be killed. We keep our weapons out, but hidden from view as we escort them. Once in the car we speed off back to the waiting plane. Everything seems to be going to plan, so far.

It would seem that our activities haven't gone unnoticed, as we approach our plane, we see a very stern-looking woman waiting for us, well-dressed and presented, I could feel her authority even before I got out of the car. Her squared-off shoulders, chest pushed out, not a hair or piece of clothing out of place. She either is or was military, not even the best jokes in the world could remove the stern look on this lady's face.

I asked Petra to stay in the car and watch the family while I go and see what she wants.

"Hannah, my name is Vera Atkins, assistant to the head of F section, SOE," she says, lifting her head slightly higher has a motion of proudness. "Firstly, let me inform you that I don't take kindly to been used as a messenger. I have far more important things to do than chase around the countryside. I am not in a good mood and I suggest you comply totally with my orders."

"Well Vera, let me inform you that this situation is one that you really should walk away from and pretend you missed us. Truly, don't underestimate our conviction regarding this matter. It might cost you your life!" I replied with a hard look back.

She paused for a moment, then passed me a piece of paper and told me to read it.

Hannah, at this time there are four snipers trained on you and Petra. They have instruction to shoot if Vera lifts her left hand. Make no mistake, they will kill you both if you don't comply.

I look up at Vera and she simply wiggled her left finger and raised her eyebrows, making it quite clear. I walked over to Petra and handed her the note.

"What's going, Hannah?" she asks.

"Read that, we have a situation."

Upon reading it, she screws it up in her fist and lifts up her sidearm and with the look of "*let's fight our way out*", she goes for the door handle.

"NO, Petra! There will be another time. We can't beat this one. Drop the weapon and slowly get out the car."

"These fuckers will pay for this, Hannah," she mumbles as she gets out.

Vera walks over and instructs the family to take the car and return home. You could see the relief on all their faces, wiping the tears from her eyes, the elder woman takes the wheel of the car. In the back seat, clutching the boy tightly the other with a trembling voice, thanks this unknown lady who has just saved them from who knows what.

Once they had driven off, Vera waves her right hand, which I assumed was the signal to the snipers to disengage.

"I don't fucking care who you people are, but..."

"Petra! Now is not the time," I stopped her before she said something we would regret.

"Now what?" I ask, turning back to Vera.

"Now you will accompany me to London. We are not in the revenge business, ladies, this is something you must try to remember," she says as her chin and her right eyebrow raising at the same time.

"Let's go. The General is waiting," she says as she walks toward the plane, gesturing for us to follow.

During the plane ride down to London, I could see Petra figuring out if she could get away with killing this woman. She didn't have to say anything to me, I could see it in her eyes. It then dawned on me, how deeply Heidi passing has affected us all. We are making rash decisions; Heidi's death has clouded our judgement, and we need to learn from this if we are to fulfil my promise to her. No matter how we move forward with this, we need to ensure we completely stay off the British radar in the future. I whisper into Petra's ear to stay calm and not to antagonise the British in any way.

"You are not British, are you, Vera?" Petra enquires.

"Romanian, actually" she replies.

"You come from money though, I can fucking smell the aristocracies on you from here," says Petra.

"Petra, how many times have I told you not to play with your food?" I shout at her in an attempt to remind her not to upset these people.

Vera simply smiled and lit a cigarette, completely dismissing Petra's comment. It was clear to me that she certainly doesn't scare easily and wasn't an ordinary woman.

We land and Vera escorts us into a car for the short trip into the city. Petra spent most of this time taking in her surroundings, as this was her first time in London. To me, it is all starting to look the same, everywhere, ruined buildings and piles of rubble with every turn.

"London has truly been hit hard, Hannah. This is some of the most devastation I have seen so far," she remarks as she continues to look around.

"Yes, Petra, but you must take some time to talk to the British. You will find they have a heart of iron."

We are taken to a different building than the one I visited before and were quickly ushered onto a staircase and we head downwards.

"Where are we going, Vera?" I enquired.

"Be patient, you will find out shortly," she simply replied.

As soon as I saw her at the airstrip, I knew we were in trouble, but I am now getting a really bad feeling about this situation, my mouth is as dry as a desert.

We are now walking down a long underground tunnel with steel doors on either side. Each door had a removable sign on the left side. They seemed to be some kind of temporary offices or something along those lines.

Eventually, we arrive at our door and Vera instructs us to wait outside. This walkway is eerily quiet, no sounds or people, just Petra and me standing alone.

After a few minutes had passed, Vera opens the door and asks us to follow her in. The room was just like the corridor, concrete and steel everywhere with two-tone walls. A little dark with only one desk and three chairs in one corner lit by a single overhead light.

It feels like we are about to be interrogated!

I did recognise the man behind the desk though; it was the General. As we approached, he simply said,

"Sit!" in a stern tone.

He was reading through a file as we sat down, while Vera pulled one of the chairs to the side of the desk and sat on it facing us.

"Do you think that we have all the time in the world to babysit you two and your group?" he asks without looking up at us.

"What the fuck is this? We're on your side, you, stupid old fucker," growls Petra.

"Oh, the infamous Petra potty mouth. You do know that you work for us and that I am your boss."

I don't usually use foul language but all I can think to myself right now is "Oh shit! now we're in trouble".

He continues. "You girls are becoming more and more of a liability than an asset, but it seems you have an angel looking over you," remarking as he closes the folder and looks up at us for the first time.

He just looks at us for several minutes in complete silence, shaking his head and occasionally looking over at Vera.

The silence is broken with Vera standing up and walking behind us, she leans on the back of Petra's chair and says: "You two could now be charged with kidnapping British citizens, that will get you, life in prison." *That doesn't sound so bad, I could do with a rest, I think to myself.* "I am sure we can also come up with several other laws to charge you with."

"They were perfectly safe, we simply wanted to question them about Otto," I replied quickly, without giving the fact away that he is still alive.

"Why couldn't you question them at their home? Where were you taking them?" asked the General.

"Nowhere, just for a plane ride. People are more responsive at ten thousand feet," Petra replied.

"So, you don't believe he is dead then?" he asks.

"Well, of that we are unsure, but we also know that he got away with thirty million when he shot Heidi," I reply, but again only giving him enough information to add foundation to our behaviour.

"Thirty million? And why didn't you tell us this sooner?" inquires Vera.

"Because they were going to keep it," interjects the General.

This was a dangerous ploy on my part. Nevertheless, one I had to take. It is better to be thought of as a thief than a kidnapper or even worse, a traitor.

"You have no idea where the money is then?" he probes.

"No, sir. We thought, find the money find the man, if he is still alive that is. If he isn't and we found the funds then at least Heidi didn't die for nothing," I respond.

"I don't want to sound callous, but we have all lost people in this war and fixating on avenging the death of your friend isn't the way forward. The war is still on, and we have work to do," he reminds us.

"Heidi's death has hit us hard, sir, that is for sure, and it is possible that it has clouded our judgement somewhat," I reply as Petra nods in agreement.

"The SOE is in the business of ungentlemanly warfare, that is our mandate. However, we are not in the business of revenge. I think it's best if we shelf this incident, but I will have no choice but to bring you up on charges if there is any more of this," he says, his voice stern.

At this point, I couldn't help but wonder why all this couldn't be dealt with in his office. For sure we have dodged a bullet and we are going to have to come up with a new method to continue finding a way to deal with Otto. My main concern now is, what the hell are they going to do with us now.

"Please follow us, ladies," requests Vera.

We head out into the corridor and turn left, two doors down we enter another concrete room but this one was different. It was well lit. The walls are covered with photos and maps. Area photos, pictures of people, names, addresses and all manner of other information.

"This information is above top secret," the General says, flowing his hand across the wall. "Over the past few months Vera and I have been working on this in our spare time."

Vera then took up the briefing. "You may recall we sent you on a mission regarding the capture of many agents in France, and their equipment."

"Yes, ma'am. It was thought that you had an informant passing their details to the Germans," I replied.

"Correct. We found that our operations officer for France was in fact the traitor and he was dealt with, which plugged that leak," Vera responds while giving way to the general.

"Double agents are a natural part of war and keeping anything totally watertight is almost impossible. Unless you keep things on a need-to-know basis." He lights a cigarette and continues. "Prior to you seeing this room, Vera and I are the only ones that know about this operation." He turned to face us. "This war is not just about killing the enemy, there is much more going on that most of us never see or even know exists. Homeland security, financial issues of all kinds, secret communications and deals are made on a daily basis."

The General provides us with a deeper understanding of some of the other issues a country has to deal with during the time of war and how complex they truly are. " Prior to war breaking out and during the first couple of years many people from occupied countries fled to Britain. Of course, this wasn't unknown to us. However, the hurdles and complexity of the procedures they have to go through to stay here are certainly concise."

I shift in my seat to get a little more comfortable, as he continued,

"The procedure is designed in an effort to weed out Nazi sympathisers and back in 1941, the British government took drastic steps to this end by interning most alien residents in camps around the island." He coughed and spat a piece of loose tobacco out before stubbing his cigarette in an ashtray on the desk. "It was decided it was far easier to treat everyone as a potential spy rather than spending days, weeks attempting to identify individuals." Opening a drawer in the desk, he removes a bottle and a glass then pours himself a drink, but doesn't offer us one. "All enemy alien residents were categorised under the (1914 Aliens Registration Act (4 & 5 Geo. V c.12) and anyone in category A was instantly arrested and interned. Category B residents were exempt from internment but highly restricted and category C residents exempt from internment and unrestricted."

I was astounded by the number of German and Austrian enemy alien residents who actually reside in Britain. Over seventy thousand of them to be exact. It also became clear to me, that with that number there are going to be many that simply slip through the net.

"During this time, it also became clear to the government that many of these individuals were active members of some of the Nazi sympathising groups of the time," he rattles on, taking his seat.

At this point Petra chips in with a few words of wisdom. "You should have saved yourself time effort and money and shot the fucking lot of them," she remarks and was met with complete silence.

"This is not just a British war history lesson, Petra. You need to pay strict attention to all of this. The reason why will become clear soon enough. I ask you to keep your glib remarks to yourself," he barks, with a shake of his head, before continuing, "All enemy aliens had to attend individual tribunals to determine their category and then each one is given an identity card providing personal details on the front and their category on the back."

He picked up one of these that had been on the desk and showed it to us. Turning to the wall, using the hand holding the glass. "On this wall are some of those people who are currently at large and possibly still living here in the shadows. What this wall doesn't show is any new conspirators they may have recruited and are actively sending information back to the Reich.

"For reasons we cannot tell you, Vera and I have been tasked to seek out any and all Nazi sympathisers in the southern part of the country. Because of the information we know that has been sent out so far, we have a good idea of where they are operating which makes things a little easier."

I find myself actively having to stop myself from yawning, the British can't half rattle on!

Vera contributed: "If we can find the lower-ranking people, they will lead us to the head of this particular snake-in-the-grass. We have sent several of our own agents down there, but after a week or so, all of them stopped reporting back."

"This obviously also tells us that we are looking in the right place. Are you ladies with me so far?" the General asks.

"So, you want us to go in and do what?" I inquire.

"Infiltrate, gather intelligence on everyone involved and report back directly to me, or Vera periodically. I need to stress that you will need to be very careful and convincing as these people are very good at sniffing out agents that we have sent in before."

Vera moves to the information wall and turns to us. "You cannot just kill someone here as it will draw the attention of the local police if you are seen, or the body is found. If you must kill, then do it quietly and make damn sure you're not seen," Vera chips in.

"Look, I am in this to kill Nazis, not play fucking spy," Petra says as she jumps out of her seat and heads towards the information wall to give it a closer look.

"We think we have a leak here in the SOE. The agents we have sent in before were some of our best. But for whatever reason, they have all been discovered," the General says.

"You two and your girls are somewhat off the SOE radar, in fact, you are only known to Falcon, Viper and us," Vera informs us, as she moves behind me and places her hand on my shoulder.

"And this is why we have no other option but to send you two in. This mission is one of vital importance and will help determine the outcome of this war," says the General.

"Also, let's not forget that you girls are earning a fortune from the Hong Kong mission currently running and you're not killing Germans on that one," Vera reminds us.

The General stands up and hands me a piece of paper with our hotel name and address and room information. Wishing us good luck, he shakes our hands and leaves the room. Vera offers to escort us to an awaiting car. I take a final look over the information wall, adjusting my dress as I do so. Sitting down for too long can ruffle your clothing, I do like to look nice. Petra and I follow Vera out of the room.

As we walk down the corridor Vera asks us, "Do you ladies need to powder your nose?"

Petra and I look at each other, with confusion on our faces, is this some kind of test question?

Vera picked up immediately on our confused facial expressions. "Do you need to use the bathroom? Toilet?" she asks with a smile on her face as she gestures toward a door.

"No thanks," we reply together and head straight for the car.

Petra and I don't speak a word on our journey to the hotel just outside of the city. We spend the journey without actually speaking, we do communicate, through eye contact and movement, head gestures, each of knowing that we are only thinking about Otto.

Ok, we have to put on a compliance face for the organisation the SOE, but our hearts aren't in this really. No question that we will complete this mission and hopefully in record time, so we can return home and regroup on our only true objective, killing Otto!

It will be good to catch up with the other girls and find out how Falcon and Viper are doing. It took almost an hour to reach the hotel, the devastation isn't too bad outside of the city. Yes, there are signs of bombing, but it isn't too bad really, the odd stray bomb crater or buildings hit here and there.

One of the things that strikes me and that really stands out about the British is their ability to just get on with life. It's wartime but you wouldn't think so watching them all go about their daily routines and chores as if nothing is wrong. We witness people cleaning windows, putting the washing out, chatting with neighbours with a cup of tea. Their resilience is amazing.

As we approach the most wonderful looking hotel I have ever seen, a brick building with a thatched roof set in a cluster of trees. We could see the sisters sat at a table in front of the building, but no Daphne.

They were deep in conversation and didn't even lift their gaze from each other as we arrived. I called out to them as we approached which seemed to startle them.

"Hello, ladies."

"Petra, Hannah. It is so good to see you. Isn't this the prettiest hotel you have ever seen?" Ellie replies with excitement.

"I was just thinking the same actually. Let us get checked in and we will have a chat," I replied.

Entering the building I almost bump into a lady on her way out. To my surprise when I look at her, it was Daphne!

"Oh, there you are Daphne. Let us check in and we will be down shortly," I whisper in her ear as I give her a hug.

A very prim and well-spoken oldish lady took our identity cards and booked us in. The foyer is quite small and they must be cooking cabbage because that's all you could smell. We are sharing a room, no issue for us, the beds are soft but the springs are very large when you move about. Petra's mind of cause goes straight to the gutter and makes some dirty comment. After checking in and refreshing ourselves we head down to the girls.
The pleasantries over, they bring us up to speed on the Hong Kong mission. The first trip has gone well. The journey is a little long and tiring though. Hong Kong is very different; the food and culture take some getting used to and there aren't many European food outlets over there. They also inform us that they have never seen so many people on bicycles before. The sights and smells of the city are something else, there is a different smell around every corner coming from different street food vendors.

The British have a good thing going over there it would seem, printing forged currency from a small backstreet service. The Chinese are great forgers,

Daphne tells me they could forge anything, this might come in handy for the future.

The girls will be doing two runs a month. This means it is going to be very lucrative to us. It's nice to hear that something is going well for a change.

We all sat outside on a large table, taking in the evening air, birds singing, the breeze rustling through the trees. We had some tea and a little to eat, some kind of stew with cabbage. After we had finished eating, had another cup of tea, Daphne and I took a walk for a chat about another matter I had asked her to look into for me.

After my first encounter with the General, I decided it was a pertinent idea to look a little deeper into this man. I asked Daphne to retain someone here in Britain, to have him followed. Prior to her leaving for Hong Kong, Daphne phoned and asked a close male friend in London to find and follow the General. It seems this came at the right time for him, he had no prospect of work due to his injuries back at Dunkirk. He agreed, but of course he wanted paying. She sent all the information we had on him, including a photo, then he set to work.

Due to our latest meeting, it seems it was a solid move. We now need leverage, of any kind, on this man. And I am hoping Daphne has some good news for me.

"Hannah, I didn't say anything at the table, but you should know. Auntie has returned and wants to see you," she informs me.

I was surprised by this news, but deeply overjoyed to hear it. "That's great news. We were all very concerned for her," I replied with a beaming smile and a sigh of relief. I felt like a huge rock had been lifted from my shoulders, joy and happiness engulfed every fibre of my body.

"Falcon and Viper send their deepest sympathies regarding Heidi. Well Viper did. Falcon simply said, its war and loss is part of that, and we should move on."

"That's Falcon for you, cold and callous," I commented, and then ask, "What news of the General?"

"I have a meeting this evening with my contact, and they inform me they have much to tell me. I will keep you updated."

We walked for a while down a small country road, lined with hedgerows and trees. The sun was setting so it wasn't long before we had to return to the hotel to turn in. Besides, it wasn't safe to walk on these roads at night, drivers could hardly see at the best of times due to the blackout on their headlights.

Prior to turning in, I call home from our room, while Petra was taking a bath. I ask Mila to let Auntie know we should return shortly and that we are all very pleased she has returned us. Mila informs me that she has brought four more girls with her and that she has placed them in the annexe. The family just keeps growing. I can't help but wonder where Auntie has been these past weeks. Grieving is a process, and we each choose our own journey, which paths to take.

I couldn't shake Falcon's words though, "*it's war and loss is part of that, we should move on*". This then brought into my mind an old Confucius saying, "*embark on a road of revenge, first dig two graves*".

In my mind, I understand these quotes, but in my heart is a desire so fuelled by loss, deception and remorse that I have to feed it. Regardless of anyone or anything, I like others, gave my word to Heidi, we will stand by those words; he will pay for what he has done.

Chapter Four
Hannah

It's 06.30 and our car is already here. We say our farewells to the girls as they are heading home to prepare for the next trip. This Hong Kong deal is every month now, which will keep them busy. Daphne informs me that although her contact has collected a lot of information on the General, there is nothing we can use.

I had a thought whilst in the car on our way back to the city; perhaps there is something we could use as leverage on him, because we need him to back off. Or a different method of attack is going to have to be used regarding the General. We will have to find something that he wants, procure it, and use that as a bargaining tool.

We collect all our paperwork including our complete backstories. I have to say that the dress code for the Land Army, is somewhat lacking in style. I guess it isn't meant to flatter in any way, but they could have chosen better colours.

We were prepared to say, our last posting was a dairy farm in Norfolk until it was razed to the ground by a crashing plane. The only upside was that it was a German bomber and there were no survivors.

We are heading for a small village called Ringwood in southern England. It's between Bournemouth and Southampton, both southern coastal cities. The farm we are going to work at has been around for over three hundred years and is owned by the Wickerman family.

The area was chosen due to its strategic position as there are plenty of military bases around there. These bases, due to them being around for a while, will provide us with intelligence. Which we can use to be passed on to the group, once we make contact that is.

It took several hours by train to reach our destination; we sat quietly and took a few naps during this time. We arrived at what can only be described as the smallest train station I have ever seen. A single building stood alone on a small flatform. The building was only accessible by the train and station staff. We follow a small group of people to the side of the building where a large-set gentleman was waiting to check our tickets before allowing us through the gate, where we are met by an elderly fellow, wearing a flat cap and muddy wellington boots. He looked at least one hundred years old, his face covered in lines, with big bushy eyebrows and a cigarette hanging out of his mouth.

"You two are our new girls, are ya?" he asks.

He spoke with a strong accent. We both struggled to understand anything he was saying.

"Are you Mr Wickerman?" I asked.

"You call me Tom," he explained slightly tipping the peak of his hat and giving a small nod. "Follow me then."

Which is what we did as Tom shuffled towards the front of the building. Staying a distance behind him, Petra whispers to me.

"Do you think he will make it home?" Petra sniggered.

"I hope so, he shouldn't still be working on a farm at his age," I replied with a big smile on my face.

"I'm amazed he is still fucking breathing by the look of him, Hannah."

Going through the gate, we are confronted by a form of transport that was almost, if not, older than the man who owned it.

"A goddam fucking horse and cart. Are you kidding me," Petra blurted out loudly.

The cart looked like it came from the eighteen hundreds. The sloping wooded sides are missing some slats. The wheels look like they have seen some miles, the metal rim has a few rusty holes, and the wooden wheel edge under it looks rotten. The horse looks quite young and healthy, so we don't have to worry about her.

"Sir, surely you have a car or a tractor for this purpose?" I asked.

"No fuel to waste on such things," he mumbled. "Jump in the back," as he taps the cart.

Thankfully it wasn't raining. And, if Tom doesn't make it, then I am sure the horse will know its way home. Luckily for us, the farm wasn't too far down the road, it only took about ten minutes before we were heading down the farm track.

The farm track with its clearly defined wheel ruts, split by a wide grassed centre, twisted and turned through the grass meadow. Approaching, we could see the large family home, an old beautiful building built in white stone with normal brickwork added at some point to make it larger.

There are several brick outbuildings and barns around the yard, which I have to say, was the cleanest farmyard I have ever seen. I was expecting animal shit and smells everywhere, but there wasn't any sign of such things, not even from the chickens. As we pull up in front of the main house an elderly couple approach us.

"Good afternoon, girl,." the lady said, helping us down off the cart by offering her hand. Petra just glared at her and jumps down off the cart herself, mumbling something under her breath.

"Afternoon to you too. I'm Hannah and this is Petra," I replied as I gathered my bags.

"We're the Wickermans, and welcome to Wickerman farm," she says, leading us across the yard. "We have converted one of the old stables for you land army girls. Hope you don't mind sharing."

The British are so gentlemanly - the man with her, her husband I supposed, never actually spoke a word but insisted on carrying our bags. Despite his age, quick on his feet and before we knew it, he was bending over and picking up our luggage and speeding off in front of us towards the stables.

As we pass a neatly trimmed low hedgerow in front of the main house, the lady picked up a large bucket of water and a stiff broom. It was only a short walk to the stables but taking us a few minutes to get there due to the lady stopping every few feet and scrubbing away any chicken droppings as we crossed the concrete. "They are necessary for eggs and meat, but I can't abide chicken droppings in my house," she says as she brushes furiously. And now I knew why it looked so clean.

In front of the stables are two old water troughs, now the home to some summer flowers, adding some nice colour to the grey concrete yard.

"Here we are then, we will let you get settled in," she says, waving her hand towards the door. "The other girls will be back shortly as Tom has just gone to get them from the field."

The couple link arms and head off back to the main house with her husband now carrying the bucket of water.

We enter our new home for the foreseeable future. It's basic but homely, with a stove for warmth and cooking and the other girls have dressed it up as best they can. There are twelve beds in this one room and not a bathroom in sight. How do we keep clean? I ask myself. I could see Petra's mind working overtime.

There are two empty beds with clean folded sheets and blankets, with our luggage placed on them, on the far side of the room. We made our beds and took a short walk around the yard. Actually, we were looking for a lavatory. No one around to ask, its late afternoon, not a soul in sight, so we went behind one of the buildings.

A couple of hours later we saw the horse and cart returning with a full cart of tired and mucky looking girls aboard. As it got closer the girls seemed very happy, contented even. Laughing and joking, giggling with each other. They all jump out and wish Tom a good evening. One of them locks eyes with me has they approach.

"Hello, ladies," she shouts as she hits the ground.

After introducing themselves and pleasantries exchanged, they made their way into the stables. I have to say, it was like organised chaos.

In twos and threes, they would strip off, while others filled a large tin bath in the corner with warm water. Depending on the size of them, you could fit at least two in it at a time. This didn't bother me at all; we had shared baths and toilets at the youth schools and the brothels. I wasn't so sure about how Petra was going to manage though. She doesn't play well with others! Surprisingly, she didn't say a word. She just shook her head and went to lay on her bed.

Instead of having to ask about toilets, one of the other girls took me next door, sure enough, there was a washroom with three toilets and several sinks. Cold water only though.

When I returned, Petra was engaging in conversation with one of the girls regarding our daily routine. Up at 05.00, ready for work at 05.30 and work until dark. I was pleased that summertime hadn't reached us yet; those days will be very long.

I informed Petra of where the washroom is situated, and she then asked the girls about food. It has to be said that these girls are making the best of the situation. They have made a large table to seat us all from whatever they could find, with hay bales as seats in one of the many sheds.

As we entered the shed, one of the girls informs us, "the food is mostly produced here on the farm, including the meat," gesturing for us to sit. It is rather a pleasant experience and atmosphere, everyone sitting and chatting while eating the fruits of their labour. Both Petra and I are asked the same type of question, where we came from, family, how come we moved to this farm. Thankfully, we already had our back stories in place.

Although we spoke perfect English, you could hear a slight European twang, so it stood to reason that we fled Europe once war broke out. Petra and I met in London, became friends and have travelled around England working together ever since. Our last position, a farm on the east coast was destroyed by a falling plane and we were re-assigned here. All very plausible, many women from Europe have joined the war effort here in England.

After our meal, which consisted of roast potatoes, cabbage, carrots and chicken, we settled in to our beds for the night; it's an early start tomorrow. The girls are chattering away about their duties for the coming days, we simply laid in our beds, taking it all in. Our first objective is going to be blending in here and observing our surroundings.

Both Petra and I prefer the short hit-and-run missions. This is going to be our first long-term mission and it's going to be a major test for both of us. It's certainly going to test Petra's social skills and probably my ability to help her keep control of her reactions.

With this many females all sharing one room as well as other amenities, it must get bitchy from time to time. Keeping a lid on our hidden skills is going to be the biggest challenge. I can already see that these girls are split into two groups, on one side are the land girls, those that work only on the land, then the others that work around the farm yard, caring for the animals, feeding, milking and so on. I see an opportunity here, Petra and I should split up, each taking a position in one of those groups.

Petra

We are four days in now and this work is fucking back-breaking. When I first saw these girls, they all seemed so delicate, oh how wrong was I. I have to say, I am not easily impressed by anyone who can't handle themselves in a fight or with a weapon. But these ladies are stronger in many ways, their stamina, they walk for miles every day, on uneven fields planting crops by hand. Lifting heavy baskets of seedlings, moving them along the trenches of the field as they sow each line. I ache everywhere. I even have muscles where I never thought I had them. Working the land is so fucking hard, I wish I had taken to caring for the animals now.

Having never really been a lady *per se*, yes, I like to look clean and have nice hair. I have the feet of a man and overly knobbly knees. I am amazed at how much time and effort these girls take to look as good as they can, even whilst on the fields. I am not sure where they find the time though; all I want to do is eat and sleep. This fucking job could be the death of me, not the way I wanted to go out!

Sunday arrives. A day off, at last. I wanted to spend all day in bed, but we are in England, it's a church day for the family and many of the girls, so they are all up getting ready. I am pleased to see that Hannah and I are not the only ones not attending. We decided today would be a good day to do some reconnaissance and start collating some intelligence on the surrounding military bases. I hate this shit; Heidi was so good at this part. We should have brought Mila with us.

Thankfully we already have as much intelligence as we need, given by the General at our briefing regarding the day-to-day stuff. We need to use that information to produce some credible intelligence that we can then use to gain good standing with the Third Reich sympathisers.

Tonight, we are told is pub night, as it's our only day off. Many of the military use the pub, so that will hopefully provide another avenue and an opportunity for me to utilize one of our other skills. Besides, it's been a while since I have felt the touch of a man. Well, one that has survived the encounter. It would do Hannah good to be intimate with a guy again, help boost her confidence back up a little. But then, she does have her scars to content with, as well as other inner issues.

No way Hannah is going to let anyone get too close to her, after that bastard Otto fucked her up. She has been hurt so deeply by him, that she will probably never let another man close to her ever again. To watch him suffer will be a great day, I understand that Hannah will probably not let me near him, she will want to do this herself, understandably!

Hannah and I spent a few hours getting to know the area. When you're going to be producing a ruse, the smallest details are everything. Creating hand-drawn maps and so forth, have to be as detailed as possible.

This area of England is quite nice and tranquil. If you didn't constantly hear the groaning from aircraft engines overhead, you would be forgiven for thinking that there was no war on. Watching the crops sway gently in wind, people on bicycles waving and saying "hello" as they ride by. The countryside is a beautiful place and a steep contrast to city life.

It's mid-afternoon now and everyone is getting ready for the pub. It occurred to me that at the rate of downtime we get, we are going to be here for fucking weeks!

We have to find these people and make contact as quickly as possible. I really want to get back to what we do best, killing Germans! I have come up with an idea whilst taking a pee though, and I will run it past Hannah during our trip to the pub. Soon everyone is ready and we start the twenty-minute walk to the pub. Hannah tells me that I am going to enjoy the experience as it's nothing like any café or bar I have ever frequented before. We hang back a little from the others so we can discuss my plan.

"You wanted to tell me your idea to move things along a little quicker, Petra?" Hannah asks.

"Too fucking right, Hannah. We need to get this done and get home as quickly as possible," I reply.

"Then do share, Petra."

"Right," I begin, "to provoke a response from others we take it in turns to disappear, on our own for short periods of time. There is bound to be someone who will notice, follow us and we then question them."

"And what if they are just nosy, all we are going to accomplish is providing many people with suspicion about us both," Hannah remarks.

"We have to do something. We can't stay here for weeks, Hannah. I am hurting everywhere and I'm very bored."

"Look, we agreed to do this, and so, we will perform our duties to the best of our abilities," Hannah says. "Your lust for blood-spilling will be satisfied soon enough, Petra, Now, let's get to work."

I love Hannah, I truly do, but her desire to follow orders can sometimes become an obstruction. It's one of her old traits from her Nazi school days that I wish she could overcome. She is more than willing to break the rules, when it suits her own agenda, but if she is given an order she will not deviate. Well, I will, and I am willing to do anything to get us out of here!

Hannah

We arrive at the local pub and Petra throws herself straight in. So much so, I have to ask her to slow down with her drinking. She has got herself involved with some airmen, who are obviously seasoned drinkers. We have only been here for an hour and a half and she is already five pints in. We cannot function if we are drunk! I remind her. Her response was direct to say the least.

"Bollocks, I can handle my drinking, and all these men. Remember, we used to do this all-fucking day, Hannah, every day."

Although I might agree with Petra that we need to complete this mission as soon as possible, if we push it too strongly, we could give the game away. We need to be patient.

The pub is full of all walks of life, from land workers to some high society folk, as well as forces personnel. Just the kind of crowd we need to get to know.

One of the questions that needed answering was the amount of US military in this pub. In fact, they outnumbered the British five to one. How come there are so many of them in this area? This had to be a question that many residents and others in the area are asking themselves. This wasn't included in our briefing, possibly for good reason. It seemed worthy of further investigation.

I pulled Petra aside to discuss this. "Have you noticed anything about the people in here, Petra?" I asked.

"Sure have. Mostly American, which works for me, as the last one I had was great," she replied with a smile and a wink.

"Petra, stop thinking about yourself for just one minute," I told her, and asked," Why is a British village pub mainly full of US soldiers and Airmen?"

"Ummm.. because there are here to help the British?"

"Yes, but where are the British?"

"Oh, yes, I see your point, Hannah," Petra replied, looking around the pub, before turning back to me. "So, if we have noticed this on our first night, then whoever is involved with the Nazi sympathisers will have too."

"Yes. So, we need to watch the areas where these US military are billeted and work. Those areas will be of importance to these people also."

Petra gulps down the last of her pint and says, "I agree Hannah, that is our path."

Chapter Five
Hannah

The walk home from pub was silent for me and Petra, but the other girls giggled most of the way home. Whispering in each other's ears, probably giving insights into their conquests from the evening. Each group walking together, linked arms throughout.

Over the next few weeks, Petra and I spend all our downtime watching and listening. Within two weeks we have established two villages of interest. Tyneham and Imber. These two villages seem to have many things in common. They are both approximately the same distance from Ringwood, a little over an hour travel time. They both have had their residents removed and are now military installations. Both are used mainly by the American forces for practice.

These are prime targets for any Nazi spies in this area. Add these to what we already know, regarding other military installations. In a radius of sixty miles from Ringwood, and now we have a major bombing target area for the Axis powers.

Although we have sent our findings to London, one thing is bothering me, why hasn't something already happened? The Nazis would be bombing the hell out of this area if they knew about it. This area hasn't suddenly sprung up overnight, they have been here for months.

After another couple of weeks, we finally find a person of interest. She has, in fact, been following our every move over the past few weeks. It's time to take the bitch down a rung or two on the ladder and hang her by my stockings.

I head off on another reconnaissance mission, ensuring she is shadowing me. However, what she doesn't realise, however, is that Petra is now following her.

Petra waits for her to settle into her routine. She, like us, had built a hidden watch den in the woods near one of the military bases.

We allow an hour to go by, letting her think she has gone undiscovered. Then, Petra makes her move; rushing in with the speed and silence of a cat. Taking her totally by surprise, Petra, pulls back her arm and knocks her out with one blow to the head.

As she fell towards the ground, Petra, raises her hands to the night sky in triumph, much like an athlete. Saying a single word as the body hits the ground with a dull thud, "Bitch."

We transport her to a nearby field away from all eyes and ears. Taking an arm each, we drag her across the field without consideration for the many thistles and cow pats. Using her body has a cushion, we take it in turns to climb over her, so we don't get caught up on the barb wired fencing. I think we must have hit every cow pat in the field, she doesn't smell very nice now and we couldn't help but gets some of that on us. Thinking about it, I wasn't too sure it was the cow pats I could smell; maybe she has soiled herself.

Pulling her off the barb wire wasn't as easy as we thought. Once we managed to do so, we could see small blood spots coming through her blouse. Only a few yards away is a tree. Removing her jacket, we sit her down against the tree and use it to secure her. Now tied to a tree we are ready to wake her. It took a few slaps to the face, which Petra enjoyed immensely. After a few moans and groans, a few shakes of her head, she started to come round. She regained consciousness, flung open her eyes as she lifted her head up. Her struggling was intense for a moment or two, then she realised that was pointless.

"What the hell is going on? And, why do I smell like shit?" she asks with a sharp tone and glaring at us both.

"Finally, some fucking fun time," Petra says, with a slight smile in her eyes. And a little grin.

It takes no time at all for our captive's eyes to adjust to the darkness. She then realises who we are.

"Before I unleash my friend on you, tell us who you are and why you have been following us?" I ask.

The woman stays tight-lipped, lifting the side of her mouth, tilting her head as she glares back at us in defiance.

"Look at her, she isn't going to fucking talk. Let me ask her." Petra blurts outs and takes a step towards her with her knife at the ready.

"No, she will tell us everything. Just stand back for now. I've got this," as I push Petra back.

I pull my knife and hold it to the throat with the tip just piercing her skin on her lower jaw. Still nothing, keeping my knife in place, I suggest to Petra that she puts some added pressure to the left leg. Petra sits on her right ankle, takes her knife and inserts the tip of her blade into her upper thigh. This technique applies just enough pain, but not enough for her to require full medical attention. She lets out a scream, the sweat now dripping down her face. She looks at Petra and blurts out, "I'm going to fucking kill you." Petra simply smiles back at her and applies with a little twisting motion to her blade.

Petra then pulls out her blade from the leg and pushes her legs apart using her own leg. Keeping them open, Petra cleans her blade on the exposed upper inner thigh. She then takes the tip of the blade and applies some pressure to the woman's genitalia. Female body parts are like male ones, it can be very painful, if you know how to hurt them.

"Ok, ok, ok, enough, my name is Nancy. I work at one of the nearby farms," she replies.

"Do you take us for fucking idiots? Tell us the truth or I will start cutting pieces of you off," Petra angrily insists as she applies a little more pressure.

"Who are you? Are you a man in disguise? Maybe you're a gutter woman? Keep her away from me, PLEASE!" she replies as she tries to shuffles back off Petra's knife.

This only made things worse for her, the movement made my knife, which I hadn't moved, cut in to her neck and pierce her jaw even further. I could feel bone now, on the edge of my blade.

"The only way to do that is by telling us the truth and nothing else," I enforce as I removed my blade from her neck. Standing up I continued, "We know you're not a land girl. Or even British, for that matter."

"Ok, ok, just keep her away from me." Glaring into Petra's eyes, she continues, "I will tell you."

Bending down I whisper in to Petra's ear, *"take a walk while my newfound friend and I have a chat."*

Petra stands up, but not before wiping her knife on the woman's thigh one more time, before replacing it in its sheath. As she starts to walk away she mumbles something under her breath.

"Gee, where did you get her from? She is one crazy German female," Nancy says has she pulls her legs together.

"German?" I ask.

"Your English is very good, but I hear small hints on some words. I thought we had removed all German sympathisers from this area," Nancy replies as she shuffles about, trying to make herself a little more comfortable.

"Removed? How do you mean removed?

"We kind of, police the area, to ensure only locals and military are resident. Any known foreign aliens have all been taken to the holding camps. So, who are you two?" she asked.

I didn't answer. I was the one asking questions here.

Made afraid by my silence and my look, she blurts out, "If you kill me, you will still be found, there are so many of us, you will not last long. You and your crazy friend have been in our sights for weeks."

I take a moment to gather my thoughts and whilst doing so, I go and find Petra. She is only a few metres away. Something isn't right, I can feel it. I approach Petra and shout out her name as I go towards her.

"She claims she is some kind of police, Petra. How can that be right?" I inform her, shaking my head in disbelief.

"Police? Did you check her papers, Hannah?" Petra asks. As she grabs both my arms, she continues, " Sorry, of course you did."

"You saw me take them out of her jacket pocket before I tied her to the tree. Her papers give her name as she stated, but why say she works on the land and then she polices the area?" I reply. "Take a look for yourself, Petra." handing her Nancy's papers.

"I will get the fucking truth out of her, Hannah," Petra says has she storms of toward the tree. I follow her, a couple of steps behind and hear "it's getting chilly out here, I want to go home, Hannah." Her thought spoken aloud.

As we returned to the tree, we realised Nancy had escaped. How? Neither of us knew, although I did make the mistake of having my back to her, which also blocked Petra's view. I had tied her up very tightly. The only way she could have got free, was with help! Her jacket was on the ground, in pieces, someone had definitely cut her free. Simultaneously we draw our sidearms in readiness, and drop to the ground. Pointing them into the darkness, we took cover behind the tree. We couldn't hear anything or see anyone, nothing but the creatures of the night happily going about their business.

After waiting some time, we make our way back to the road that leads back to the farm. Constantly checking behind us and around corners and shadowy areas. Slowly and very carefully, we make our way back to the farm.

We also realised that we are now the hunted; they think we are Nazi sympathisers. It might be time for us to get out and back to London, and quickly!

For the rest of the night, we took turns sleeping in shifts, just in case. However, it turned out that it didn't matter. As the morning broke our door loudly was kicked open. At least six armed men and women rushed in. Through the hysterical screaming girls, they pushed one of the girls to the ground. This caused another chain reaction. These girls are fighters, I'll give them that, but no match for these well-trained individuals. Through the continued high-pitched screams, you could hear the occasional bottle breaking and the sound of wooden furniture hitting the walls as the intruders made their way towards us. Taking a quick survey of our situation, there was no way out, no real room to fight due to the close proximity of the other girls, I didn't want them getting hurt any more than they have been. We decide it was prudent to simply not resist. As the intruders dragged us off our beds and started heading out, I could see the full force that they used. The room was totally destroyed, a couple of girls had minor head injuries. They have stopped screaming but their faces said it all.

Dragging us out of the barn, all the other girls are asking them, what we had done, in high-pitched voices. The intruders never responded, simply keeping their weapons pointed at them, huddled together like sheep in a pen.

Entering the yard, we came to a sudden stop. The old farmer was stood there, shotgun at the ready, pointing towards them. Not actually ever hearing him speak before, his voice is very distinctive, very low tones and gravely. "What are you doing on my land?" he asks.

One of the female intruders walked right up to him, flashed their ID card and stated, "Suspected Nazi sympathisers, sir. We taking them in for questioning." She then turned her back on him and instructed the men holding us to put us on the back of the truck.

Petra and I managed to stay silent. I couldn't help but think this was about to be payback time for us both. The woman we questioned last night was the one giving the orders, and she didn't seem happy at all. I recognised her voice instantly.

Blindfolded and tied up we are thrown to the floor of the covered truck. The engine started; I for one was now attempting to find out our direction and destination. Through the silence of all those in the back with us, I could hear tractors groaning in fields, birds chirping and squawking. It wasn't difficult to work out our direction, there aren't many roads around here, and Petra and I have travelled on most of them. We are heading in a northerly direction; it seemed like we are going to one of the many US camps situated north of the farm. Every noise, every turn, Petra would nudge my knee with hers, a sign she was doing the same as me. We stayed completely silent for the whole trip.

After what seemed like an hour or so we arrived at our destination. Interrogation resistance training is part of everyone's training, I guess, we are about to find out if that training actually works.

I think they have taken me into a building. They untied my hands and re-tied them to a chair. Still blindfolded, I could make out several voices. Darkness and voices are for the time been, my only constant. They are discussing the best course of action.

Without warning, I felt a thin wire around my neck and I started to struggle for my life. The pressure in my head increased immediately as the blood flow was cut off. I felt blood start to stream down my neck as the wire is tightened. I could no longer swallow due to my throat closing up. This is it, it's my time. But, through all this, I couldn't stop the question in my head *"why are they simply killing me?"* and the stupid things that go through your mind as the end closes in, like, *"How will I hide this scar, I can't grow my hair to the shape of my neck."* None of this mattered, I will be dead!

That wasn't their intention, they just wanted to let me know that they could kill me, if they wanted to. It was just the beginning. They remove the wire and my blindfold. In between the coughing and spluttering, I gulped down as much air has I could. It's amazing how people forget how precious this life-giving force is. We never really think about it, until it's taken away from us. I felt a sharp stinging sensation from a strong slap in the face. Although painful, my eyes were adjusting to the light in the room, that was until the slap. Now I was trying to see through a flood of tear fluid.

"Wer bist du wirklich und wer ist dein betreuer?" the female asked me, *"who are you and who is your handler?"* in almost perfect German.

I could tell, from their voices, that all in the room are American and that they think we are Nazi sympathisers. My eyes now adjusted. I was in a darkened room and all I could see was my interrogator and a table she was lent up against in front of me.

"I am not the person you think I am," I replied still coughing and spluttering for air, in English.

"You are German, that we can tell for sure," my interrogator shouts, slamming her hands down on the table. Leaning down towards me, now at eye level, she continues, "Why are you not in an internment camp with the rest of the alien residents?"

Someone grabs my hair, twists it down to my skull, and if that wasn't painful enough, they then wrench my head backwards. I instantly felt the wound on my throat tear a little wider open. I couldn't see them due to the light above casting a strong shadow over their faces. The man held tightly and growled at me, "You're going to tell us everything. You just don't know that yet."

"Again. Who are you and who is your handler?" the woman repeats.

I could hear screams coming from a nearby room. It was Petra and by the sounds of it, she was resisting too. After each scream, Petra, would laugh at her interrogator, a good tactic, I wish I had thought of that. That must have frustrated the hell out whoever her interrogator was. I could hear the distinctive sound of skin meeting skin has they continually slapped her, in the face, I guessed.

I was preparing for the next round as my interrogators regrouped. Then, out of nowhere, a loud vibrating noise filled the room, a darkened shadowy figure stood in the now open-door way.

I could hear a male voice but couldn't quite make out what was said. However, judging by the face of the woman in front of me, she knew who he was. She spun around on the spot and made her way over to him. Still unable to hear a word, this didn't look good for someone in the room. I still couldn't make out who this man is, she was blocking my view. I saw her pushed to one side and heard him growl angrily, "Release her at once!"

Without hesitation, someone from behind me untied me. As the man came into my line of sight, he says, "Please accept my apology. Hannah, isn't it?"

"Who are you?" I ask as I rub my wrists and throat.

"Please follow me. We will get you both cleaned up while I answer your questions," he says as he helps me out of the chair.

I now know we are on a military base, judging by the wall colouring. Which one, I had no idea.

As we enter another room, I saw Petra being treated by a nurse. She had several small facial cuts where she had been punched. The nurse asked me to sit, telling me someone would be with me shortly.

"Who the hell are you people? I know you're American," I ask as I am treated by another nurse.

"We are OSS, and you are SOE agent's, yes?" he replies.

"We aren't telling you shit!" Petra snarls aggressively.

I nod in agreement.

"Ok, I understand. Tell them nothing, straight out of the training manual. We will do this another way then." He asks the nurses, "Have you finished with their wounds?"

"Yes, sir," one of the nurses replies as they leave the room.

"Right, come on. Let's get going," and he gestures for us to follow him.

Outside, we all get into a car that was waiting and before I could ask where we were going, the driver asks him, "London sir?"

"Yes, and don't waste any time."

Chapter Six
Hannah
May 1944

A few hours later, we arrived at SOE headquarters. Maybe he is on the level after all. In any event, we are about to find out what is going on, I hope.

As we walk in, showing his ID he requests an immediate meeting with the General. We are all ushered into a room, tea and coffee promptly arrive. A few minutes pass and an orderly opens the door and asks the man to follow him. We find ourselves left in the room, sat with the female OSS agent. It isn't just the room we share, now; it's also the torture and the scars that come with it, it's also the ones that we have inflicted upon one another.

The room echoed with the sounds of fluttering paper has I glanced through the newspapers and pamphlets. I sat myself back down next to Petra on the other side of the room to the OSS agent.

"I am sorry about how we treated you in the field," I said to the OSS agent. There was a slight moment of silence which was broken by Petra "Well, I'm fucking not."

The room was filled with an awkward silence once again. For a few seconds, we just looked at each other. I could tell she was weighing up how to respond.

"As I am for your treatment back at the base," she replies as she stands and scans the posters around the room. "Neither of us knew at the time who we were or who we worked for. Let's just move forward, hey?" she holds out her hand, waiting for me to shake it.

Hours go by and we are getting hungry. The awkward silence was broken by Petra, "These fuckers need to think about feeding us," she blurts out. The agent takes the hint and goes to ask about getting some food. Another thing I have noticed about the British, they never rush anything. Bloody stiff upper-lipped, well I want to get my lips round some food! *My thoughts can't seem to get away from the fact, I am hungrier than I thought I was.*

Lunch time comes and goes. Around 2pm, some sandwiches arrive, Oh, and more bloody tea. It's then I realise that the agent hasn't returned. Has she gone home? I wondered.

"Will they be much longer?" I ask the orderly as he places the tray down.

"No idea," he replies, swifty, quickly exiting the room.

Petra lifted a sandwich with distaste and showed it to me. "Well, these sandwiches are as dry as fuck, Hannah. Honestly, I have seen more life in a fucking limp dick."

We have been sitting in this room for most of the day now, and quite frankly, I for one am starting to get a little fed up. Not to mention totally bored; there is only so many times you can read the posters and leaflets in the room. Some of them are rather interesting though. They have one called " Dig for victory". This leaflet outlines how to prepare the ground, how and when to sow the seeds, to grow your own vegetables. I was seriously considering taking it; it may come in handy at home.

They had leaflets and posters for everything: reclaiming, metal, paper and cardboard. Even one on "Make Do And Mend It", step-by-step instructions on how to mend your clothing instead of throwing it away. I must have read these leaflets at least four or five times by now, I am getting bored. Each one of them has a number, but it seems has though some are missing as they don't run in sequence.

The silence is broken once again by Petra, now pacing around the room, "This is getting ridiculous Hannah. They better hurry up or I am fucking off." Petra is getting agitated with the current situation; she isn't one for just sitting around.

We have heard footsteps and phones ringing all day from behind the closed door. It's early evening now, and the hunger has returned. Still no sign of anyone from either side. What can be going on, why is it taking so long to sort this out?

Finally, the door swings open and in walks a different orderly. Petra, lunges for him, but before she could do or say anything, I hold her back with a simply hand gesture. He jumps back, startled by her reaction, possibly due to he has no idea how long we have been in this horrid room. Gathering himself he then says, "You have been ordered to come back tomorrow morning."

"Are you fucking kidding me? You bastards have had us in this room all fucking day." I look back at Petra, with a simple lift of an eyebrow, a tilt of my head, and I ask her to calm down.

Ignoring Petra's outburst, he continued, "We have organised somewhere for you to stay overnight. Please follow me to the car." He turns around and starts heading for the door. Petra's frustration gets the better of her once again,

"What the fuck is going on?" she shouts at the orderly, swiping all the leaflets off the table. This stops him in his tracks. He turns and looks down at the floor, now littered with the leaflets. He tuts under his breath in disgust, he starts to clean them up. I bend down and help him. Placing the leaflets back on the table, I decide I will keep a couple of them. The orderly heads for the door once again.

Shaking his head in disbelief at Petra, "Shall we, ladies?" gesturing towards the door. I didn't need to look at Petra, I knew she was going to do or say something else, so I just held my hand up in a stop motion.

Our lodgings turned out to be some damp, dingy bunker. Filled to the brim with families. It did not help that we were serenaded through the night by the bombs, either, resulting in little sleep. Even underground you could hear the whistling from the Germans bombs. The sudden explosions which could be heard, and felt, even underground. The ground would shake, dust and brick would fall from the ceiling. Quite unsettling even though we'd been through this before.

I moved onto Petra's bed and held her hand tightly. Neither of us spoke, she knew why I was there, she simply put her arm around me.

"I have got you, Hannah, it will be over soon. Try and get some sleep." Covering my ears with her hands.

We didn't get much sleep, people coughing and snoring pretty much kept us awake for the rest of the night. The smell of unwashed bodies lingered in the air. At times, I could taste the dust and sweat.

In the morning, I woke with Petra still holding me close. She does have a kinder side. She just doesn't show it to many people. We put our shoes on and head for the exit. For me, seeing the daylight and feeling the warmth on my skin, I am aware of the tension releasing from my muscles. I let go of Petra's hand and took in a few deep breaths. Petra's response was somewhat more simplified.

"Well, that was a hell of a fucking night. Next time we get an invite to visit London, I'll give it a fucking miss, Hannah."

We stand around looking for the car to return us to HQ. Whilst waiting, it occurred to me that we didn't know the OSS agent's real name. And, where did she disappear to yesterday? We had, after all, l spent a few days getting to know each other in one form or another, so it might be appropriate to introduce ourselves properly at some point today. That is if she is there.

I hardly have time to finish my thoughts and the car arrives. It comes to a stop next to the bunker entrance, out of the passenger side jumps the agent, smiling and clearly unaware of the night we had just endured.

"Morning ladies, shall we go, busy day ahead," she shouts across the car and jumps back in.

"Hey, isn't it time to introduce yourself, instead of us having to use your false name?" I ask as we walk over.

"Ummm...not sure, I will have to wait until I get permission to do that," she says, with a smile on her face.

Bloody American's, they are almost as bad as the British. Always having to do things by the book.

It's a wonder either country ever actually gets anything done in this war. Every " T" has to be crossed, every " I" dotted. I wonder if they use the toilet by the numbers; one, two, three, push!

Now, back in the same sodding waiting room, tired and in need of a bath and some fresh clothes. We start pacing the room, occasionally giving each other a surly glance, and Petra, mumbling under her breath.

At least we didn't need to wait too long, fifteen minutes, in fact. A female orderly asks us all to follow her. I already knew where we were going, we had taken this route before; we're heading towards the General's office.

The smell of stagnant cigarette and cigar smoke filled the room. Four men had already commanded the space, buttoning up shirt sleeves and replacing their jackets. It seems like they had been here all night.

I spotted the General, but I didn't recognise any of the others.

"What the hell is going on, General?" I ask.

"Ladies, please sit. At this point, the only person in this room you need to know is the gentleman sitting to your right: Major Colby of the American OSS." The General, gestures with his hand, pointing him out.

Major Colby was a short, balding fellow with a chubby round face, wearing dark-rimmed glasses perched upon his nose.

"Well, that's very nice, but what the fuck does that have to do with us?" asks Petra in a frosty tone.

"I will thank you not to use that language in my office, young lady," the General replies in a stern voice, before continuing, "Your operation in the south is cancelled. We have a new mission for you. Over to you, Major."

"Ladies, what I am about to tell you is top secret and cannot leave this room. I am heading up a special force and the General has informed me that you ladies should fit right in."

"Oh, and why is that?" I ask with a flippant tone in my voice.

"You have already proven that you can handle interrogation, that we have now witnessed firsthand. However, the General has shared with me some of your more, let's say, colourful exploits over the past few years". The Major gets up and walks over to the table in the corner and pours himself a coffee. He then continues, "You have local knowledge and have worked with the French resistance on more than one occasion. You also speak several languages and you're both qualified to parachute. It's also clear, you don't mind dangerous missions. So, with that in mind, we would like to send you both up to Scotland for two weeks special paramilitary training."

Petra and I immediately turn and look at each other, Petra gives me a little nod suggesting I reply.

"Well, that's very nice. We already have the necessary training. If you know so much, you would already be aware of that. Why do you deem it necessary that we need even more training?" I ask.

"Look here, ladies, you will go where we send you, without knowledge of why at this point. And, you will, do it on that basis," grunts the General.

I could see Petra was aching to reply and, I too was somewhat intrigued as to why we would need more training. After all, killing Germans was our main forte. If they want to make us more efficient at that, then so be it.

"You can get your travel information from the orderly and I suggest you get some rest on the train; you're going to need it, girls," instructs the General, indicating that the briefing is over by pointing towards the door.

"Right then, off to Scotland we go," I reply as Petra and I rise from our seats and leave.

We collect our belongings and tickets and head for the train station. This is going to be a long day; I for one was not looking forward to several hours on a train with a tired, angry Petra.

For the first couple of hours, we both just slept, waking periodically and taking in the scenery. I was shocked at how many towns and cities were war prepared in northern England. Men and women in uniforms of all colours, bomb shelters and even some bombed out buildings could be seen at every stop.

The British stiff upper lip mentality never ceases to amaze me though. They are constantly living in fear of bombs and been sprayed by machine guns from the attacking planes. Nothing stops them laughing and smiling. Children are playing in the fields, housewives are still going about their chores, putting the washing out

At the same time there are those that just sit quietly, contemplating, perhaps their losses or maybe a loved one on the front lines. But then there are those simply going about their daily lives, men and women chasing each other, those who have already found love, kissing and cuddling.

Love is possible and does happen in occupied Europe. However, most people are far too busy now trying to stay alive. Scurrying for food and not been killed by either the Germans or now the allied forces. People over there spend their day searching the skies every day and night for planes. We often see people searching for a safer place, hundreds, if not thousands of them. We pass them by and watch as they carry their last few belongings has best they can, fear, is at the forefront of everyone's mind over there.

After several hours, and a quite a few train changes, we finally arrive at the coastal town of Arisaig, Scotland. We are met by a very serious looking sergeant, who made it very clear from the start that we shouldn't be here. His gaze was one of distain, his face tightened and his lips folded inwards. His head shaking side-to-side has he looked us over. His stance, like a statue, not a piece of his uniform out of place, he opens his mouth and we are greeted by a gravelly voice,

"You two, with me," he grunts.

He proceeds in full British military fashion, so rigid, marching along the streets so proudly. The residents must be used to seeing him because it seems like we are the only ones noticing him. He escorts us to our lodgings, well, it's more of a scurry for us -yes, he is rigid but he can move at a good pace.

Turning right and lefts through the town streets we arrive at three white stone-built homes, which it seems, is where all supposed volunteers for this two-week training, will be billeted.

The sergeant then instructs us of our time table, "You will be up, dressed and on the waiting truck every morning by 06.00 hours. If you're late, you will walk." He spins on the spot, slams his right foot down as though on parade and takes his leave.

The next morning at 04.30 we are up, dressed in British army battledress, male ones naturally, as we are the only females on this training course. They are made from a woollen fabric, brown in colour, the jacket has two pockets, one on each breast and a button-down front. Whilst the trousers have a large map pocket on the left leg and a single pocket on the right. They are oversized for us both, we had to make some makeshift belts out of cloth, to stop them falling off our hips. Thankfully, the sleeves had buttons on the wrists, we both looked like we had added a few pounds.

After getting something to eat, with the rest of our squad we climb into the back of a truck waiting outside. After ten to fifteen minutes, we arrive at a very secure area. Armed guards at the entrance and eight feet tall fencing surrounded the compound. Every face is screened and every name checked off, which took much longer than the drive here.

We are herded into a large room and ordered to sit down. Usually, when there are twenty or so people shoved together in a room, there would be a bit of idle chatter going on. Not here, though; everyone's sat in silence, eyes fixed to the wall or watching each other. We're doing the same thing - surveying the room and the people in it, taking in impressions of our new companions.

After what seems like minutes, a door swings open and we all jump off our seats to attention. In a single line, three men, each wearing a look sterner than the last, filter into the room and make their way to the front.

"Be seated," the first guy orders.

One by one they provide us with their insights regarding the training we are about to undertake. No introductions, which was strange for the British. He simply goes straight on:

"Over the next two weeks you will be physically and mentally tested. We are going to push your minds and bodies to their limits and beyond. You can leave at any time, you will not be judged and it will not be entered onto your record."

He takes his seat and gives way to the second man:

"You can call me Doc, everyone does. Because we use real weapons here, I will be seeing many of you, of that, I am sure. If you sustain a major injury then you will be removed from the course."

The last man then gave a full thirty-minute briefing of the training schedule, and safety briefing, which consisted of the following:

Cross country Hiking/Running,

Ten miles every day. Must be completed in under three hours.

Hand to hand combat,

Four hours training every day. To include instant-kill knife training.

Pistol training,

Two hours daily range and moving target practice.

Safety. All he had to say about that was, don't get shot or stabbed.

At the end of the briefing, Petra learns over to me and whispers, "What the fuck are we doing here? We have done all of this, twice before!"

"Just go with the flow, Petra. Because, boy, are they in for a shock," I replied, a little smile on my face.

Everyone collected gear and off we went on our first hike across the Scottish countryside. It is very quiet here, and the views are stunning. You had to watch your footing, though; one wrong step and it could be all over.

An hour and a half out and the same back, with nothing to show for it but a lot of sweaty bodies and blisters on our feet. We decided to show the guys how this is done, we hiked out but ran back. Every guy we pass shouting at us, "Are you crazy, slow down, it's not a race." We are determined to show these people we have just as much right to be here as they do. The blisters on our feet put Petra in one of her moods, muttering under her breath and shaking her head, but it was worth it.

After a little lunch and surprisingly a choice of tea or coffee, it was time for hand-to-hand combat training. First, they tire you out and give you blisters, then they beat you up to top the day off.

Our trainer for this afternoon's activity was the serious-looking sergeant from last night. The one that thinks we shouldn't be here. That was his first mistake. His second was picking Petra for the demonstration.

"Right lassie. You're first," he growls, pointing at Petra.

I hope they have a medical facility here; they're going to need it. Petra made her way towards him, her eyes dark and her mouth twisted in an angry scowl.

"Well, now. You think can train like a man, do you?" he barks at her, his neck veins bulging out, as he steps in close, so close in fact their noses almost touch. "Shouldn't you be at home, making babies and cooking?" he snarls again, right in her face.

Stepping back, looking over at the rest of us with a twisted cruel smile. He then makes what can only be described as a half-hearted lunge at her. With that, she grabs his arm, steps in and throws him over her shoulder.

His body hits the ground with a loud thud. His face was a picture, reddened with surprise that was followed by shock and then understanding. His lips were pressed thin, his eyes wide and unblinking. The sergeant's expression was only surpassed by the ripple of gasps that surrounded me. They each turn to look at me and, you could see it in their eyes: they have underestimated us, and now they're unsure what to make of Petra and I.

The sergeant got up, brushed himself down, the shock slipping from his face, and I could see that he was resolved to change his approach. Grabbing each other's arms, they wrestle around in an attempt to get one another off balance. The sergeant uses his strength and pushes Petra backwards, Petra was ready for this though. She grabs his clothing and, in one move, drops to the ground bringing him with her, pushes her feet onto his stomach and flips him over the top of her.

The guys give out a loud cheer and round of applause as she quickly gets to her feet. It seems they have found a new respect for the pretty ladies. The sergeant gets back to his feet once again, Petra now in a ready stance, but instead of charging at her, he walks up to Petra, holds out his hand. Petra waits a moment, unsure if this was a ploy for an arm lock or body throw. She takes his hand, but still in a state of readiness, in case she had to counter, giving a slight nod in respect as he shakes her hand.

As she walks back towards us the guys part like the sea, making an opening for her has she returns to my side.

"Fuck, that felt good," she said to me as she sat back down with a smile on her face.

I simply nodded in agreement. After a few minutes of watching the others have a go, I eagerly await my turn. Man, or woman we can always learn something new. Some of the arm lock holds they are using, are new to us and deserve practice. Has we continued to watch we are tapped on the shoulder and asked to report to the main office.

Standing up and brushing ourselves down the others turn their heads away from the training and stare at us, you could see it in their eyes. They are thinking exactly what we are, what is going on? We make our way off the field, giving each other a silent glance every few steps.

Entering the main building, we are instructed to wait by the captain's door, against the wall. The orderly knocks and waits for a reply. " Enter" the captain shouts.

"The trainees you requested, sir," says the orderly.

"Send them in, corporal," we hear the captain say.

Standing in front of the officer, his face, a curious colour of purple, his eyes opened wide, glaring at us. He proceeds to go on a what could only be described as a sermon. I glance over at Petra, and from the look on her face, like me, she isn't listening. I for one would rather be outside getting thrown around rather than listening to his voice. Periodic slaps upon his desk echoed in the room, which made me pay attention, until he finally pulled out some papers. Our files, I can only assume. This continued for several minutes but it seemed longer than it actually was. He paused, stared at us both and asked, "Why aren't your files up to date?" He yells, his spit foaming in the corners of his mouth, occasionally flying across his desk. "And why weren't we informed of your training?" he snarls with an angry glare. "Just who are you two?" he continues, prodding at the file, so hard I thought he would punch a hole through it.

"We have nothing to do with what's in our files, sir. We were simply told to report here and that is it," I replied.

He sits down at his desk, places his clasped hands to his chin while he contemplates the situation. I glance over at Petra, who is staring back at me, and I shrug my shoulders before returning my focus to the captain. This has to be quite the situation for everyone concerned. For the first time in their lives, they are confronted with two women that could actually kick their asses.

A few more minutes pass before he stands and walks around to the front of his desk. Takes his Colt pistol from his side holster and hands it to me.

"Strip and re-assemble this for me," he orders.

With only seven components, the Colt 1911 pistol is quite easy to strip down. With quick release buttons already built in, the pistol itself is easy to strip down in the field, no tools required.

I press the button next to the trigger and the magazine pops out into my right hand. Then at the business end of the barrel, I press another button being careful to keep pressure on it because, if you don't, it will hit you in the face as its spring-loaded. I twist and rotate and remove the barrel bushing.

Next to removing the slide: I line up the marks on it with the notch on the pin. My hands now feeling a little greasy from the weapon's lubricant. I cock the weapon by pulling back the slide; it should now be lined up with the first notch. On the opposite side there is another button, I push it and the pin pops out. This is so easy, I can do this with my shut, in fact, we train all our girls to do exactly that.

Now the spring comes out and I remove the slide. Job done in well under one minute. To re-assemble, I simply do everything in reverse.

"It's clear you're no stranger to firearms," the instructor says.

"That's correct, sir. We are all fully trained on current sidearms and knives," I reply.

He looks between us disapprovingly before returning to his seat. "Total waste of my time, bringing you two here. Pack your belongings; I am sending you back to London and be assured, I will be putting in a call to HQ prior to your arrival."

"Ok, sir," we reply, heading for the door.

Leaving the compound, we dash back to our lodgings before he can change his mind. We pack our stuff, collect our tickets from the station and, within the hour, we're on our way back to London.

Our journey back to London was a quiet one. Petra and I simply looked at each other, my smile mirrored on her face. It was as if we were thinking the same thing: "We showed them."

It must have been difficult for the men and their fragile little egos, to come to terms with what happened. In our line of work, one should never disclose your training history. If they had known, then they might have been aware they were standing in the presence of two women, both of whom had already killed more Germans. than the lot of them put together.

We had now spent more time travelling than we had doing anything else. For me, it had become quite tiresome. Thankfully, we arrived back at HQ, but where it quickly became apparent that waiting around was the order of the day, while we would have rather gone for a bath and a good, stiff drink. Two hours later we are back in the General's office. Major Colby was the only one in the room.

"Ladies," he says whilst pacing the room. "It seems that you didn't last very long in Scotland."

"Total waste of our fucking time. We are already better trained than any of those men, and we proved it." Petra, snaps.

"You missed the reason for the exercise," abruptly. "You weren't sent there to train; you were sent there to see if you could take orders. Which thankfully, you did. In an effort on my part to make things more difficult, I purposely withheld your full background from the training officers." I for one couldn't believe this, all that was a test, well, personally I think we aced it.

He continued, "I told you at our last meeting that the General had given me everything on you girls, including your lack of respect for the chain of command."

Right, so not a great second impression. I had to disagree though. "Sir. We have been on several missions to date. The only missions that we have failed are due to them being cancelled at the top, either that or down to bad intelligence," I firmly state.

He drew himself up. "I am fully aware of that, but that doesn't concern me. What does concern me is your running side missions without authorisation, disappearing for days on end and making your own targets for personal gain. This war isn't being fought so you girls can get rich on it."

Here we go again. I wanted to inform him that the money didn't matter, that we are in this to stop the tyranny of the Third Reich. Our motivation is pure and simple: Survive by any means. Steal from those that have already stolen - and in most cases, killed to acquire their gains - an eye for an eye. Furthermore, it's not just about Petra and I. To date we have helped so many other girls, and given them a safe home as well as a new purpose in life. But I knew in my heart he wouldn't get it. So, I needed a different approach if we were going to appease him.

"We have both witnessed first-hand how brutal the Third Reich can be. Our parents were taken from us by them, killed in cold blood. We have been taken from our world and used as prostitutes for their own gain. Stripped, hit and abused by these men. You question our motivation?" I stare into his eyes for a swift second in an attempt to gauge his thinking. Then I continue, "You will never find two people more motivated to rid the world of these tyrants. Hatred runs in our veins. Our hearts beat only for revenge, and we will not stop until they are all removed from power or until every last one is no longer walking the earth." Taking in a deep breath I feel Petra's hand tighten around mine, giving it a little shake, just to let me know she is there with me.

Colby starts sifting through his paperwork. His expression remains flat, I wish I knew what he is thinking. He proceeded to hand us both a sheet of paper and a pencil. On the paper is a list of fieldcraft training. He asks us both to put a line through those that we have already had training on.

~~Parachute Training~~
Demolition
~~Physical Training~~
~~Map Reading~~
~~Field Craft~~
Aerial Re-supply
Anti-Tank Warfare
Street Fighting
Intelligence Gathering

This only took a few seconds to complete. He examined the amended list, puts the file down and stares at us both for a moment. His lips tighten, he nods his head and then goes on to say, "Right, I am sending you both to Milton House near Peterborough. We need you to be fully up to speed on the rest of this list."

"This is a waste of our fucking time," Petra snaps her hand away from mine and sits up sternly in her seat. She continues, "We don't need more training to kill bastard Germans..."

Interrupting her, "Insubordination will not be tolerated from either of you. You will go where we send you. At this point you're not required to know why, simply that, you go where we send you, when we say."

He called the meeting to a close with "This time I will send your training requirements ahead of you to save us all some time. I will see you both back here in about a week. You will then receive your mission briefing."

Chapter Seven
Hannah – The Training

Milton House is a very large and beautiful stone building. I guess the British are in some ways, not too different than the Third Reich. If they need or want a building, they take it. Surrounded by large grass areas and woodland scattered with bunkers and large sand-bagged areas, this old mansion would truly be a beautiful place if it wasn't for all the military men and equipment.

Although we had to sleep on canvas cots surrounded by men, we were designated one of the main building's bathrooms, so at least we had a little privacy. However, there was still no change on the wardrobe front; men's battledress once again. Here we go then, let the fun begin. Demolition training today. Predominately railway sabotage.

The instructor heads off into his spiel: "The Third Reich relies heavily on trains to transport almost everything they require. Troops, supplies; even food. So, causing as much disruption to these lines would have a great impact."

We learn that plastic explosives are the preferred material for causing maximum damage to railway lines. 'Explosive *Nobel* 808' has always been a go-to charge for the SOE. However, now they have an even better version called ' RDX Composition C-2'. This version was far more stable in extreme temperatures, C-2 is a mixer of 80% RDX and 20% plasticizer.

This two-hour instruction is quite interesting but I can't wait until we start actually blowing things up.

"I hate these long fucking lectures," whispers Petra in my ear.

The instructor continues, "To de-rail a train, simply place two charges on the inside of the track, wait for the train to come by, press the plunger and boom."

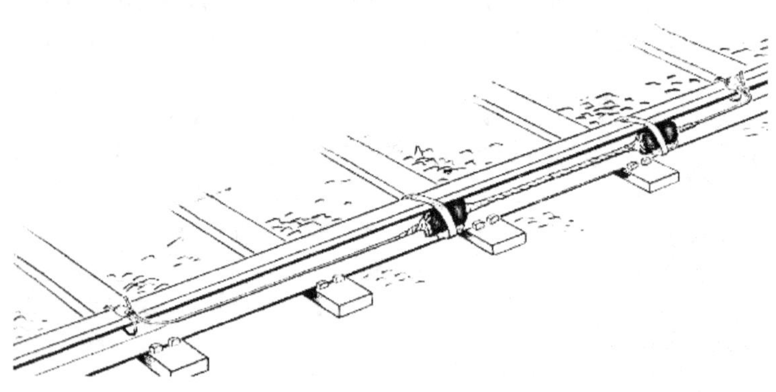

Well, hello. Been there, done that, but one of the fascinating things about this stuff is that you can just about mould it into any size, large or small, and you don't need much of it to produce results, so forgive the lesson as we learn about this more powerful material.

We stop for a little lunch. It has to be said that both Petra and I are a little excited right now, this afternoon we get to actually handle this explosive and in the words of Petra:

"We're going to blow some shit up."

Not as much as we would have liked but, even in the small amounts we were allowed, great results.

The afternoon training over, we head back for a little clean-up and get ready for dinner. Some kind of stew was this evening's choice. Not really sure what we are served though, it looked and smelt like dish water to me, plenty of vegetables and hardly any meat. After finishing our meal, we head straight off to bed.

The next morning was a repeat of the day before; get up, get dressed, have breakfast, and get ready for the day's activities. What a great day yesterday, we actually had a little fun learning about and using the explosives.

Today is all about 'Aerial Re-supply', which we are told is critical to any mission. According to our instructor, without material support, a mission could fail. Well, we have already proven them wrong on so many occasions regarding that statement. Best I keep this to myself though, don't want to hurt their egos.

The instructor continues on with his lecture. "Since May 1943 the OSS have actually been delivering agents and supplies into occupied Europe in a clandestine manner."

Ok, so they have been doing this for a year. They should be pretty good at this by now," I thought to myself. I continued taking notes.

We are also informed that they now have a facility here in Britain, capable of re-supplying over 100,000 fighters with arms, ammo and explosives. He continued to explain that they have over sixteen modified B-24 bombers dedicated only to re-supply. I couldn't help at this point to wonder, what the hell is going on? The two major questions in my mind now are, where and why?

Back to the instructor, who now shows us the two different types of cannisters they use for the drop and he then explains: "There is the " H" type and the " C" type.

The 'H' type once landed can be unclipped into five segments, each segment is easily carried by a single person. A standard load for this type of cannister would be, five Sten guns with fifteen magazines, one thousand rounds of nine-millimetre rounds, fifty-two grenades and eighteen pounds of explosives. Each cannisters total weight would be 281 pounds including the attached chute.

"The 'C' type is used for the larger weapons, such as rifles and sub-machine guns. Once each container is loaded it is packed with shock-absorbing material like Burlap.

This is a sketch I did of the " H" type.

"How do you determine the drop sites?" I ask.

"Good question," he replied and continues, "All drop sites are determined by the people on the ground. They must be kept away from towns or cities. As secluded as possible with at least a small clearing." He takes a swift glance around the room, maybe checking we are all still awake. "Once a request comes in, it will be processed, packed and loaded onto the plain. A few minutes prior to the drop, the ground team will use what we call the 'S' phone." He picks one up off the table to show us. "These are short-range ground-to-air radios which are used to contact the pilot and guide him into your drop zone. If no radio is available, then a flash light or flare can be used."

Placing the radio back down on the table, he went on to explain: "Once your position is determined, the pilot will drop down to between four hundred and six hundred feet at an almost stall speed - one hundred and thirty mile per hour - and deliver your supplies, and then head for his next job or head for home," he explained.

After the lecture, we spent the rest of the day familiarising ourselves with the cannisters and the equipment they could carry. We packed and unpacked a section each.

Once lunch had ended, and uneventful, I have to say. We had a little time to spare before our next session, so, I took a short walk around the grounds and had a couple of smokes.

It was then time for 'Anti-Tank warfare training'.

Another dismal classroom day having to listen to some old guy prattle on, and more note-taking. We are instructed to bring plenty of paper as there will be not handouts in this class. Personally, taking on a tank as a foot soldier, isn't something I relish.

A brief description of a tank's defences was given. A forward-facing machine gun on the turret, another machine gun and the main gun, which can only fire in the direction it's facing. One of the other issues with the turret gun is that it can't fire any higher than twenty-five degrees; this means if you're higher than this in close quarters, they can't hit you. So, high roof tops and or high embankments are ideal for tank ambushes.

Both Petra and I are actually transfixed; these are the types of training sessions we need. We both enjoy learning about new tactics and weaponry.

The training rooms are really nice. Loads of dark oak wood, and some truly beautiful old furniture, but these metal framed canvas seats are horrible on your behind. After taking a quick gulp of tea, the instructor continued, "The tank also has about a twenty-degree dead zone around them". With a large pointing stick, he references the large diagram to his right. "If you can get inside this zone then you can cause some real damage."

"That's all well and good, but how do you stop a tank?" someone shouts.

"There are several methods available," replies the instructor, unfazed and confident.

" Smoke grenades. Throw one in front of the tank and it will stop. Throw another behind it and now you have a static target that can't see a thing. Placing tins across a road will cause the tank commander to stop his vehicle; he will need to investigate as he has no idea if they are packed with explosives. Even placing blankets across a road on string or rope will be enough to make them stop to investigate. Any kind of obstruction will stop a tank, then simply move in and do your worst."

I couldn't believe this; tins and blankets will stop a tank. *"Surely not,"* I thought. Then Petra leant over and whispered in my ear, "What a load of fucking rubbish. No way that would work on a Panzer driver."

The instructor went on the provide us with some attack weaponry. It is a good job we have brought plenty of paper; by the end of this session, I might have almost written a full chapter from a book. Our instructor continues and we all keep scribbling down. Normally, during these types of training sessions, I have time to draw a few sketches, but today isn't one of those days because there is so much to take in. The room echoes with the instructor's voice and shuffling paper, only interrupted by the odd cough, or someone lighting up a cigarette.

"Once you have stopped the tank, you can either use a rifle grenade or Molotov cocktail. The rifle grenade is, as its sounds, fired from your rifle. It will bore a hole through the outer shell and send bursts of hot metal into the tank, killing everyone inside. A Molotov thrown onto the engine, located at the rear of the tank, it will burn and will find cracks, fuel and oil and will just keep on burning, even into the tank."

Petra and I knew about Molotov cocktails. Created by the Finns against a Russian invasion, a bottle containing a mix of petrol, paraffin and a little tar or similar to help the mixture stick to its target. Originally, they would light a rag stuck in the neck and, when the bottle broke on impact, the mixture would explode into flame. They developed a method of replacing the rag with windproof matches and keeping the bottle sealed, not full though, as that aided breaking. This was deemed safer for the thrower.

Our instructor was talking. "Tank armour is thickest in front and on the turret. The top, sides, rear and belly of a tank have thinner metals. These are your target areas for rifle or rocket grenades." The instructor pauses once again for a gulp of tea. "Another weak point on the tank is of course their tracks, wheels and cogs. Here we have a few examples of tank track disabling," pointing to the diagrams behind him.

There isn't time to sketch these though. I'm also sure that this instructor has done this many times, because he has an orderly bringing him a constant refilled mug of tea to keep his whistle wet (as we have heard the Brits say).

"First the anti-tank mine - place on roads, open terrain, farm tracks. You can also fasten three or four of them together with rope or string. Then, wait in a concealed hiding place and when the tank comes close enough, pull on the rope to bring the mines under its tracks. Then you have some options to take out the personnel.

"Now, a well-placed grenade will do the same job as the anti-tank mine, but remember you have to get in close enough to be effective. The same can be said regarding the 'Sticky Bomb', or the S.T. Grenade." He lifted one of these from the table; I thought it looked like an old rag covered in black mud. We all momentarily looked up, then it was back to jotting down more notes. "These are coated with a sticky substance, placed on a wheel or track of a stopped tank becomes a very effective tool."

"What the fuck is a wooden log doing on the table? That's not going to stop a tank" Petra shouts.

"That's where you're wrong, young lady. Please join me up the front," he says, motioning for Petra to stand by his side.

At the back of the room behind the blackboard and diagrams is a mock-up of a tank track, complete with drive cogs and wheels. It has a handle attached to one of the cogs, which will turn the tracks as if its moving.

He instructs Petra to get ready on the handle. The wooden log is about two and half feet in length with a diameter of about twelve inches. He walks around the back and places it between the rear drive cog and wheel.

"Now, try turning the wheel," he instructs Petra. While she tries, he explains, "If you have run out of mines, grenades, all other equipment, then this is an effective method to prevent a tank from moving. The commander will have no choice but to investigate. Then you can pick him off with your rifle and spray the inside with gunfire."

"What if they're travelling on open ground or, say through wooded areas?" someone asks.

"We will discuss that further after a short break," the instructor replies.

I, for one, was pleased. My hand was starting to cramp due to all the writing. Why they didn't make a booklet or handbook regarding this training, I will never understand.

Every one of us are standing, walking around, shaking our writing hands to restore them and getting cups of tea. The break only lasts fifteen minutes, until the instructor returns and asks everyone to take their seats.

"What if they're travelling on open ground, or say through wooded areas? One of you asked. In most of these cases, they usually have their hatches open. The trick here is to get them to button up. You again have several options in those circumstances. If the commander is stood in his open hatch, then shoot him, this will make the others close their hatches. Or you could take a shot at the personnel through the open front hatches. Both will have the same effect."

They have gone to all the trouble to make these diagrams, which our instructor has constantly used throughout the session, so why on earth haven't they made them smaller to hand out to us. Anyway, back to more writing; I'm going to need another pencil at this rate.

"If they are travelling with hatches closed, go for the periscope or vision holes glass. This will virtually blind them to the outside world. You are then able to use any of the tactics available and discussed earlier."

He takes another sip of tea and continues. "Always hold your fire until the tank is well within your range, until you see the whites of their eyes so to speak. Never - again, never - run directly in front of a tank; you will only make yourself an easy target."

"If you're in a fox hole, you're pretty safe. However, be ready with a stick bomb just in case they go over the top of you. Finally, always work in teams of two or more. One to get their attention and another to attack from either side.

"That's the end of our session today, take the next hour to come and study the boards and devices on the tables." Packing up his notes and placing his empty cup on the tray, he heads for the door, turns and shouts, "And remember: Seek, Strike and Destroy" were his final words to us.

There isn't any actual field training after this session, but then I guess they can't afford to keep blowing up their own tanks. We each take our time to move around the tables, examining the items. We even had a go on the tank track using the wood to disable it. It seemed to work in the classroom, but I am not sure how it would work in an actual battle atmosphere.

We grab our lunch and go outside to find a quiet spot to eat. It seems we all have the same idea; after being cooped up in a room together all day, the fresh air and open outdoors seem to be calling us all. Petra and I manage to find a spot under a tree. Whilst eating, I attempt some rough sketches from the training, but my hand was stiff and ached so much, I just couldn't do it. I gave up and lit a cigarette instead.

With no more training due for now, we use the rest of the day to relax, taking a stroll or reading a book, some even a take nap or two.

We get up early the next morning and straight into the morning routine - training starts at 08.00.

Now, street fighting tactics; this isn't something that we have ever used, nor can I see any reason to do so. We're more of a strike and move force. Oh, and let's not forget, stealing as much as we can, in as little time as possible.

Today is more classroom work, taking notes and then onto the actual field assessment. The first thing our new instructor, a young man not in uniform, informs us is, there isn't any need to take notes if we don't want to. The booklets on our tables have all the information in it. This was a relief to us all.

He then gets straight on with it. "Do not stand right up close to a window. Stand a couple of steps back, or far enough back so that your rifle isn't sticking out the window. Thus, not giving your position away too early." (*That actually made a lot of sense to me*). "If you're using a machine-gun, spread a carpet or sheet down first, then place the weapon. Another simple yet effective method is to wet the ground under the weapon and keep it wet. This will help prevent any dust clouds which may also give away your position.

"In street fighting, never cross a road unless it is necessary. Instead, always progress on the same side of the street, moving door-to-door one at a time and never bunched together. If someone is hit, keep moving. Do not attempt a rescue, for by doing so you are giving a sniper another potential target."

"This seems very basic to me; it's the same when fighting in a wooded area," I say quietly to Petra.

Petra leans in and whispers, "But if you're hit, Hannah, I'll take my fucking chances. No way, I am leaving you."

The instructor continues, periodically wiping the blackboard and drawing a new diagram whilst he talks.

"Building clearing. Whenever possible, a building should always be cleared from the top down. It is easier to throw grenades down the stairs, or down through holes in the floor, than it is to throw upwards. Upon coming across a closed door, one person holds the door handle, while another gets a grenade ready. Then open the door, throw the grenade in, quickly close the door. Once the explosive has gone off, enter the room, anyone not killed at this point, will be suffering from a concussion from the blast. Making them an easy target."

"Now that's what I am talking about Hannah." Petra whispers to me, with a disturbing smile on her face.

"When performing building clearances, work in two teams, one clearing and the other covering, picking off any threats."

The instructor gestures over to two soldiers to start. They demonstrate this using the small but effective mock-up room.

The instructor then went on: "If possible, always have another team clearing the buildings on the opposite side of the road. Keep communication open at all times, moving up the street as one unit. When moving from one building to the next one, never move together; the team on the right should move up first, while the other team covers them. Then, take up a covering position and signal the second team on the other side of the street to move up." (*This sounds a very effective method and should help minimise casualties, I think*). "Whenever possible, use smoke grenades to provide cover while moving up a street. If the enemy fire is too intense, or they are too heavily dug in, use mortars to aid in the dislodgement of their position," he says, picking up a smoke grenade and then placing his other hand on a mortar sat on the table.

And that was the end of that session, right on time for some lunch and a few smokes. The afternoon was spent practising throwing all types of grenades and a hands-on for the first time of mortar operations.

The evening was mostly spent going through the hand outs and booklets we had collected.

All next day, we spent practising these tactics in some old abandoned houses on the grounds. Both Petra and I found this so much fun; we have always preferred the practical over classroom stuff, and blowing things up was one of Petra's favourite things to do.

The following day, it's back in the classroom, but one saving grace is that our week is almost over. Intelligence gathering is our training session. Instantly my thoughts go towards Heidi; this was one of her favourite things. It was a good job that I had Petra here with me; I missed the first thirty minutes because my mind was fixed on my dear friend. I miss her!

The basics of the missed information was that, at no point should any papers be kept on a person in the field regarding their activities. This is not only to help keep the individual safe, but anyone else they are working with. If documents are to be kept, then they should at all-times be coded by the use of a cipher. If it is necessary to transmit information, then that information should be written down at the last possible moment and then transmitted. Always destroy the paper afterwards.

I have now, come back to the room, but I am struggling to keep my mind on the instructor's words. The room keeps blurring in and out, my memories of Heidi keep playing in my mind, like one of those talking pictures. Each frame cascading into a clear vivid scene. I see her laughing, then crying in pain, laughing again on our lawn at home, the sun, glistening, through her blonde hair. My mind is flooding, I just can't stop it.

I don't think the instructor has noticed; Petra had though, I felt a sudden but sharp slap on my arm. "Where have you gone?" she asks.

I tuned in to the instructor's lesson. "The information that should be collected consists of the following: Identification, location, strength and movement of enemy troop units. Aircraft, material, supply dumps and the like. Any defensive positions, gun emplacements, type, size and range, age and condition"

"Should this be referenced on a map, or just pieces of paper?" someone at the back asks.

" A map whenever possible; you should always be carrying a map in the field. If you lose it or it's destroyed, then use anything you can find. Furthermore, fortifications, blockades, pillboxes and trenches should also be noted. Minefields, roadblocks, tank traps, communication and transport facilities should be included."

"Why are we having to know all this?" I ask.

He was not put out by my challenge. "Everything will become clear once you return to your units and given your mission objective." He looked round the room. "Now, if there are no further questions, I will move on.
"If near a shore line, then intel on the location should be gathered. The terrain behind the beach, roads leading out from that location inland and any fortifications and troop activity.

"Regarding airfields, runway length and construction, obstacles surrounding it, hangers, fuel and oil supplies, communications, connecting rail and roads. Of course, any defences should also be noted.

"It is very unlikely, but just in case. Secret weapons and bases, any and all information should be noted regarding these installations. Location, sources of supply, camouflage, production, defences."

"Moving onto paperwork. Any and all kinds of papers should be collected and returned to your chief intel officer as soon as possible. The type of papers of special interest would be travel permits, identity cards, rationing books. Further information regarding their correct use, should, whenever possible, also be gathered."

"Who is the chief intel officer?" Petra asks, the same question had occurred to me.

"You will be informed of that when you return to your unit. Now, please, no more bloody interruptions; I have another class in a few minutes." Obviously, his patience had been tested enough as he slammed his hands down on the table in front of him and glared like an angry big cat about to attack.

"The relationships between the local civilian population and the occupying force and local police should also be noted.

"And lastly," (*and I thought I hear him sigh*), "any intel gathered, should at all times be transmitted back as soon as possible. This is vital; never think, it can wait an hour, because by then, it might be too late.

"That's it for this class. Don't forget to take your booklets and study them. Thank you for listening."

I, for one, am glad this is over. One more night here and it's back to London tomorrow for our final briefing, hopefully we will find out what this is all about then. Maybe now we can get back to what we do best.

We spent a few hours in the bar, just relaxing, and, as was usual, Petra had to fill an urge. Within an hour she was in the arms of some guy she had taken a fancy to. As for me, although a few gentlemen tried, I made it quite clear that I wasn't interested. For me at this time, Otto was the only man I was thinking about, but not in a pleasant way. His presence in my life came at great cost to us all. His day will come, and although I am fully aware that his death will not stop the pain and empty feeling I have deep inside, it will, bring me great satisfaction.

The next morning, we caught the first train back to London. The journey was quite pleasant; the sun was shining and everyone seemed in good spirits. Upon entering the city limits, it looked like London had been hit again last night; once off the train and walking to the HQ on Baker Street there were still several buildings burning. The air is thick with the smell of burning timber and dust, choking us with every step and breath we take.

We have returned to the Waiting Room, where more tea is served as we hang around. I am craving a decent cup of coffee. Fortunately, we were not left idle too long and an orderly opened the door and instructed us to follow him.

Instead of going to the General's office, we are escorted to a large briefing room. As we entered, I noticed guards on both sides of the doorway. Four guards? This seemed a little excessive to me at the time. In the room are about twenty other individuals, all here for the same briefing. Some of them I recognised from the training course. Whatever this is, it's going to be big.

Colby, the General and several other officers walk in and close down the room. The chatter stops and everyone stands up in total silence.

"Morning, all. Be seated," Colby instructs, before getting straight into his spiel. "This is a top-secret operation, one that will without doubt, strike at the very heart of the Third Reich," he begins.

Petra and I glance at each other with an approving look and nod. We're going to get back in the thick of it, at long last.

Colby was still talking. "This is 'Operation Jedburgh'. Your mission: to drop behind enemy lines and provide as much help, training and assistance to the French " Maquis" or resistance for those who don't recognise that term. You will lead sabotage and guerrilla warfare attacks within your given areas. You will organise and arm the local resistance, identify and set up supply drop zones, procure intelligence and set up liaisons with allied personnel."

"What are our targets for sabotage?" a solemn faced man asks.

"Your targets are to be determined by your team leaders. Once contact has been made, you will divide into groups of three. You will cause as much mayhem and destruction as you can. Each team will be equipped with the Type B mark two radio, sabotage gear, weapons and ammo."

"Excuse me, Sir, the radio, that's the B2 yes?" Petra asks.

"Yes, or, as we like to call it, 'The Jed set'," almost cracking a smile, before continuing. "Each team will have 100,000 francs. This money is to be given to the resistance personnel in your area and help them purchase weapons and ammo and other supplies. In addition, your radio operator will have a further 50,000 francs for additional costs."

Maybe that's why the SOE are counterfeiting money in Hong Kong; if each of us are a team leader, that adds up to two million already. There are plenty of others going through the training, too, they're going to need all the money they can get hold of.

"Right, once your name is called, follow the orderly for your individual assignments. That's all, and to each and every one of you, don't forget: Surprise, Kill and Vanish."

I do have a little giggle to myself when they come out with these mottos. Do they have a special team of people making these up? I couldn't help but wonder.

Petra and I were called first. Into the General's office we went.

"Ok, ladies. Because you already have established contacts in France you get first pick of your areas. You each will lead your own teams, select a radio operator from your area and a second in command from the resistance," the General instructs us.

"When do we leave, sir?" I ask.

"Straight away. Your equipment and money are waiting for you at the airport. Good luck and good hunting," he replied, showing us the door, eager to get to the next team.

"That had to be the quickest briefing I have ever been through. They seem to be in a big hurry with this one," I said to Petra as we exit.

Chapter Eight
France

Our drop was a night one, which was no issue for us. Once on the ground, we buried our chutes and head off to make contact with the resistance. As far as we are aware, that's at least twenty teams, dotted around in different areas of France, with the same mission objectives. Success will all depend on the strength of the resistance they find once contact is made. The French resistance strength can be a little as three or four members, up to over one hundred in other areas.

Now, we are not stupid; the Allies are planning something big. As for where and when, who knows, but it has to be near this area of France, or what's the point to us all being here? Unless we are a diversionary tactic, draw attention to us away from the main objective. 'Ours not to reason why...'

Within a couple of hours, we make contact with our resistance friends. The death of Heidi had trickled down to them; they knew her well and were sympathetic. Once we got past the inevitable awkward moment regarding Heidi - hardly anyone could look us in the eye, they simply walked past us one by one, either placing a hand on one of our shoulders or hugging us - we set to work. First things first: Prepare our drop zone and get our supplies. This was established in short order and the supplies are on their way.

Second objective: Split into teams which will be quite a few as this group is a large one, which will determine our targets. Both the resistance and ourselves know the area well. They already had intel maps showing us every military base, road block, check points, fuel and supply dumps. This did make our job a little easier, but all these targets needed to be confirmed. I requested that the resistance leader sends out runners to confirm all targets and numbers at all these locations. We also required information on all trains coming and going out of this region.

Thirdly, we required all SOE radio operators in our area to be collected and brought in to the camp with their radios.

Now, it's simply a waiting game for the supply drop.

Meanwhile, one of the resistance unit commanders had a map of the railways system for the area. Studying it, we decided to concentrate on Alencon. The town had several lines coming in to it; the main line was from Paris which came in from the south. Also from the south are Le Mans and Tours. Attacking this line would cause the most disruption, as it would cut off three main cities. Approximately thirty miles North East are two more main lines coming in to the area from Paris. Those two lines would also be targeted.

Intelligence showed that Rennes, Nantes, Tours and Le Manns would require targeting due to those having military bases, check points, supply dumps and further valid targets.

Splitting into our teams of three, we will have almost fifteen teams. That's a lot of havoc scattered over a large area. Each team will stay and perform hit-and-run tactics within their given zone.

Each team will be re-supplied via air drop, so, they must first determine a safe drop zone and send the co-ordinates up the chain. I had a thought on this matter; It would be far safer to get a re-supply prior to any attack and, once the drop is made, take the supplies to an established safe area. This way, each team is less likely to become an easy target for the Germans. This was agreed by all concerned. Now, it is time to collect our first supply drop. We took ten men with us to provide perimeter cover.

June 5th 1944

The supplies gathered and distributed, teams ready to go and in their given zones. It had been agreed to co-ordinate our first attacks, which is to be at 02.00 hrs. This will hopefully make the Germans think they are being attacked by a very large force over a greater area.

My team was called 'Reds' while Petra's is 'Tigers'. All the other teams are given either male or female French first names. I had to ask if anyone in my team knew why we're called 'Reds'? Fortunately for me, one of our guys is a fan of US baseball and he quickly brings me up to speed. 'Reds' is short for 'Red Sox', a major league team in baseball.

I could never understand these types of games, nor the British fixation on cricket or the US on baseball..

It was still early in the morning, to be exact, 01.00, and I could hear in the distance the sounds of aeroplanes, lots of them it seemed. As I listened, the sound grew louder, as more and more came within earshot. Then, out of the blue, the planes' roar was drowned out by the loud thudding sounds of explosions coming from east of our position. It was all over the radio - the Allies are bombing Normandy. That was it, I thought, that's why we are here. The Allies are coming.

Then, more radio chatter; they are also bombing Calais and parts of Northern France. In fact, the bombing there is far more intense than that at Normandy. It then occurred to me: It is extremely possible that the Allies are sending out false messages to confuse the Germans. If the Allies are coming, then they will not want to give away their likely landing site. With this in mind, they are simply bombing the hell out of the Eastern coast line. Quite clever, really.

After a short period, I could actually see the planes in the distance as they did their turns for home once they had dropped their payloads. It was the Allies all right, and way too many planes to count.

Our first target is the train station in the town of Alencon itself. The lines in the south and east of the town are also going to be hit, but taking out this main hub will cause even more disruption. We prepare our charges - there are two lines coming into the station - so we set charges on both, just for good measure.

The 'Tigers' are deployed a little further north of our position. Their first objective was to take on the 21st Panzer division. Using anti-tank weapons and explosive charges, they are to cause as much mayhem as they can. The 21st has approximately one-hundred and twenty-four tanks. The fuel supplies and roads are also to be targeted, but not any main routes in or out of towns or cities.

Other teams deployed also had similar objectives regarding any tank divisions in their given zones of operations. We still had no idea what was going on, but, according to our gathered intelligence through the resistance, there are now some ninety-three teams of 'Jeds' operating up and down the whole coast of France. These teams stretch as far North as Dunkirk and in the southern towns surrounding Rennes.

02.00 hrs is upon us, and like a well-rehearsed theatre production, fuses are lit and we take cover. At first, all we could see and hear was our own explosion and the destruction caused, followed by the whistles and shouts of the German soldiers scurrying about in the mayhem. But once the darkness took back the night, we could hear and see flashes of light and distant booms from other attacks in the distance. We retreated quickly and quietly and moved on to our next objective, which was checkpoints and supply dumps.

Our next objective was 'Forte Domaniale De Bourse', a large munitions depot. It is approximately fifteen kilometres from our current position of Alencon. By our estimation, this depot holds over fourteen hundred tonnes of munitions. However, we are certain that by now, the Germans are on high alert; so, we must be careful.

Firstly, we have to make our way to the objective. En route, we are coming across small groups of German patrols, taking out those that we consider easy targets, working round larger units that could delay us or cause us to take casualties.

The depot is now about ten kilometres out from our current position; that's another couple of hours or so of walking, depending on what we run into on the way. We make good progress along our chosen route and, before we know it, it's the start of another day - the sun starts to rise above the horizon. We have to be even more careful now, as we no longer have the cover of darkness to aid us.

06.00 sees us arrive at our next objective. From our last lot of intelligence, they only had a small contingent of men guarding this depot. However, because of all the attacks now taking place we are facing a much larger force. We spilt up and take new positions, enabling us a better view of what we are now up against.

From my new position, it was hard to get a realistic count; but I have already counted up to the mid-fifties. Our team rendezvous at the agreed time and place, and debrief our findings, and after a short recap, it is agreed that we must be dealing with at least half a company of men. That's about one hundred and twenty soldiers; they certainly aren't messing about now. This is going to take some assaulting, and a great deal of planning, if we are to survive. It was decided that our best plan would be to wait for the cover of darkness, and then two of our team will sneak in and plant explosives on everything they can. We will use ten-minute fuses, allowing them time to escape the compound.

So, for now, we will retreat back into the woods and build a small hide. A hide is usually built for the purpose of contacting advancing forces, and providing actual field intelligence. Our purpose is simple: using the surrounding brush and trees, we will build a makeshift hideout so we can get some rest. Of course, we will do this in cycles, always having one of us on guard.

It's times like these when your head starts turning to thoughts of others. I couldn't help wondering how Petra is getting on, and Otto was never too far from my mind. As I took the first watch, I had plenty of time to construct some pretty awful ways to end that man.

" Setting fire to his genitals."
" Nails, hammered through his hands"
To mention just a couple from a long list.

I use my time taking stock of our food and ammo as a distraction, but that didn't last too long. One thing is certain; we will require a supply drop before sunrise tomorrow.

Again, my mind drifted. I was thinking of home; The tranquillity of the estate, the smell of fresh bread in the morning on the breakfast table. We haven't returned there for several weeks, and so I pulled out my trusty pencil and decided to do a few sketches to help pass the time.

I haven't seen the boys in weeks, but this is how I remember them looking. Strong, playful and, by now, exceptionally well trained by Christa. I guess I am missing home more than I thought. Every morning, they would lay or sit outside the front door ready to greet me hoping for a little treat.

Before I know it, that's my watch over; time to get some rest as it's going to be a long day until nightfall. That's how the rest of the day continued; six hours of sleep and then three hours of standing on watch. Eventually, the daylight gave way to dusk.

We left our hide around 20.00 hours in search of a decent drop zone, and it wasn't long before we found one far enough away from the depot as not to be seen by them. The message was sent and, in a few hour's time, we will be re-supplied.

Waiting for dusk to become real night, we prepared for the depot attack, getting everything ready and hiding what we didn't need to take with us. Catching us by surprise, our 'S' radio sprang to life, startling us all. The correct codes are uttered, and ten minutes later, we had our supplies. We unpacked them, pushed the cannister and chutes in some thick bushes and started off for the depot.

We're heading off back towards our target, cutting telephone lines and taking out any checkpoint as we progress when we hear the sounds of people moving in the woodland; it seems like they are heading in the same direction as us. I send one of our team to investigate who they are and their strength. If they are German, are they searching for us? We had no choice but to wait for our scout to return.

It didn't take too long, but he wasn't alone; He had another resistance fighter with him. He gave our single (friendly approaching) sound as he approached. Once they came into focus, I could see that it was a female he had with him. Has there been some confusion, I thought, was there another Jed group working in our area? As they got closer, I could tell she was limping. Had she hurt her left leg?

"Hello, Hannah. My name is Maria. Or, as you may know me better, 'The Limping Lady'," she said quietly.

"Of course I know you. Your picture is everywhere, the most wanted spy in Europe. I thought you were dead or captured?" I replied as I shook her hand.

"Most certainly not dead, and never captured. I had to move north though as the south had become a hot spot for me," she informs me as we kneel down to help cover our position.

"I am sorry to say this, but you're much older than I thought you might be. The pictures of you must be very old ones?" I asked.

"Oh, you mean this?" she said, and proceeded to pull at her face until parts of it started coming off.

I nearly throw up; it looked so real as she peeled off her face. Then she explained; she has a movie makeup friend, who made her a disguise so, she could return to Europe. The resistance group she was sent to work with didn't like taking orders or instruction from a female, so she organised her own group and has been working independently ever since.

We also discussed our target, and it seems we are both going after the same one. It was agreed that with a much larger force, more damage could be done and far more Germans can be killed. So, that's what we did. After all, she had a force of over thirty resistance fighters with her. I would have been a fool to turn her down, not to mention having the chance to work with such a legend in our field.

We continued onwards and joined her group. I was surprised to see that almost half of them are female. The way they moved showed how well she had trained them, moving like cats stalking prey through the woodlands, silent and in a state of readiness. I was also surprised to see how agile Maria was, even with her prosthetic leg.

Once at the depot, she instructed her people to surround it. She then turns to me and said, "It's your show. Deploy your team and we will follow in behind you. Remember, kill everyone in a German uniform."

I didn't hesitate for a second. Within a few minutes, the fireworks started. Explosions going off, gunfire from every angle; they were like a well-oiled machine. Maria's fighters took up positions to cover every doorway and shot anyone who came out. My team continued planting explosives on anything and everything they found.

The bullets whistling through the air, the sounds of ricochets coming off metal and concrete, men screaming in pain, are quickly drowned out by the sounds of explosions. Each time a bomb went off, everyone ducked for cover, providing a respite for those still in the fighting.

In less than ten minutes the whole show was over. We collected any documents that seemed important, as the rest of them cleared out every other room, ensuring we left no one alive. It all seemed a little anti-climactic after the excitement of first attack.

We returned to the cover of the forest a couple of miles away and made camp, and had a well-earned cup of coffee. Maria and I sat and chatted for a short while, until she took her leave. She had informed me that they are roaming around, taking out anything they come across. Much like our teams. She did agree with me on my thoughts that the Allies are coming; it was just a case of when, and where.

We had picked this spot to make camp, due to its proximity to our supplies that we had hidden earlier. We cleaned up the camp and headed off to re-supply and then decide on our next target.

All night long we could hear the low rumble of plane engines echoing through the night sky. The Allies sure are giving the Germans hell right now; these planes are much further inland than the others were. No bombs dropping, though, maybe they can't find their targets; or maybe they are supply drop planes we are hearing.

It was decided to get an hour's rest before we move on, though. It also meant it would be light by then.

Chapter Nine
June 6th 1944 06.00

We woke to a misty morning in the forest. Checking our map, we had a short two-to-three-mile hike to our next target. One of our guys had not slept all night, he was fixated on all the radio chatter that was going on. He also seemed in a very jubilant mood this morning.

We headed in an easterly direction; this target was, in fact, on our secondary list, which we would only attack once we had taken out our first three main targets. It was a small billeting area, used as an overnight stop over for any German units travelling in that direction. But it was too close to us to miss it.

We are only thirty minutes or so into our little hike when, in the distance, we hear some very loud big gun noises. It was so loud in fact, that it was echoing around the sky.

It could only be the Allies; they are here.

We all smile and rejoice. If this is actually the Allies, then this is going to be a big day for all of us in France. This notion quickened our steps, it was like we were given some kind of high energy kick. However, we could be wrong, the Germans could be simply testing every big gun on the east coast defences. Just for the hell of it.

As we approached our objective, there seemed to be all hell breaking loose. Everyone, even some partially dressed or getting dressed men, as they ran to their vehicles are shouting something in German. I get a little closer so I could hear what they are saying.

"Die Verbündeten sind hier." (The Allies are here) over and over again.

They are frantic, speeding off in every direction and in any form of transportation they could find. We decided to take out as many as we could, as they mounted their vehicles. Firing and moving as we went. This did prove to confuse them for a time, until an officer took control. He organised his men and we ended up in a firefight. Bullets flying all around us, first the sounds of them whizzing through the air, then wood cracking, falling small branches everywhere. We're pinned down.

This tactic proved a little foolish; I was hit in the shoulder and my comrades, both were shot and killed. If it hadn't been for the German's more important engagement on the east coast, and the fact that I had stopped returning fire, I am sure they would have found me and finished me off. While the remaining German's regrouped and sped off to reinforce their coastal defences, I laid my comrades out, best I could, marking their position on my map. I collected what I could carry and moved off in an easterly direction.

It was now confirmed though, the Allies have arrived and it seems the Normandy coast is in fact their chosen landing point. I started to make my way towards there when I was approached by a British paratrooper, who very kindly took me to see their medic. On the way, we exchanged a few words.

"So, you're one of the friendlies we were told to look out for, then?" he asked.

"Yes, dropped in a few days ago. How come you are so far behind enemy lines," I asked.

"We're here to secure some major targets. that's all I can tell you," he replied.

"Well, good hunting and good luck," I said, as we arrived at the medic station.

The bullet had gone straight through my shoulder. It would be sore for a few weeks but the medic told me it would be fine. He patched me up, asking me how I ended up being shot, so I told him it was a stray bullet.

I requested to speak to the commanding officer and the doctor ordered an orderly to escort me. Upon my arrival, I saw several brawny looking men huddled around a map. The orderly made them aware of my presence and then left me standing there until I was called over.

I knew that all commanding officers are fully aware of the 'Jedburgh' mission and, of course, they had a list of all groups working in their areas. I was beckoned in and asks how he could help. I responded with the pass phrase *"the sun is shining and the future is bright."* He immediately cleared the area of everyone under the rank of captain before giving his response *"Those who dare, will surely win."* He asked me for my team's name and to show him on the map which area I was working in.

I marked my area, and also the objectives that we had hit and destroyed so far. I went on to mark out on his map anything of interest from my area that I knew about. He brought me up to full speed about what was going on and I handed over all the intelligence we had gathered over the last two days or so.

I requested he provide me with a weapon and supplies so I could get back to our main hideout and regroup. My request was denied, mainly due to my injured shoulder. He ordered me to stay in their camp and await medical evacuation.

It's time now to look after me and the sisters. They are my only concern now, let the Allies do their job. Besides, I am no use with my arm in a sling.

The Allies have amassed the largest force anyone has ever seen and are currently landing on three of the Normandy beaches. Hearing this filled my heart with joy as I wandered around the camp looking for the radio station to see if they could contact Petra's team to make sure they - or she - had made it.

After spending a few days with these British paratroopers, I was evacuated with other injured soldiers back to Britian. They had set up large field medical units on the south coast. As we flew over Normandy, I could see the enormity of the force that had landed. There is the biggest gathering of ships I have ever seen on the sea, they stretched for miles, as did the smaller craft ferrying the troops to shore. It was the most spectacular thing I have ever seen in my life. Those of us that could look out at this never to be seen again spectacle, cheered and shouted, *"give them hell, boys"*.

As soon as we landed, we are transported by army ambulance to the medical tents. After we had been checked out, we made the journey to Portsmouth Hospital, one of the main medical facilities for injured troops from Normandy.

After a change of bandages and a clean sling, I was able to ask about other women in the hospital. I had to find out if Petra was here. I also made a call to the General to see if he had heard anything. But, unfortunately, he wasn't available as he was very busy right now. The orderly did however tell me he would make the necessary enquires and find out what he could and ring the hospital back if he found anything out.

I was starting to get a little worried. I had to find Petra at all costs. Everyone I talked to was just so busy, no one seemed to care about one woman. Ok, I get it, they had bigger problems than one missing female to deal with. To me, though, she isn't just anyone, she is my sister, the only family I have left, she is the only one I am bothered about. Of course, yes, I have the other girls and auntie is back in our lives, but Petra and I had been through so much more together.

I spent the next few days wandering around the female wards, checking every bed and looking at every intake, and everyone leaving. Still, there was no sign of her. I had even rung home and asked them to make every effort to track her down. With no success.

After a couple of days, I was given the OK to leave. I headed straight to a plane bound for home. During the journey, I read a newspaper. It seems the Germans are putting up quite a fierce response against the Allied forces. Losses are mounting fast on both sides. Over four thousand Allied troops lost their lives on the first day alone. We are now on day three, so that figure has surely risen, that is for sure.

I feel in my heart that Petra is not one of those who has paid the ultimate price of war. It might seem silly, but it's the only way I can stay calm; if I think even for a moment that I have lost her as well, my stomach churns up, my mind goes to mush and my heart feels like it's going to explode.

Within a few hours I am landing in Switzerland and met by Daphne, who was taking a short break from the Hong Kong mission, in order to take me home. There was still no word on Petra, but Auntie and the other girls are all doing well though, she informs me on the way.

It was great to be home again and to spend some time in a totally safe environment. Having my own bed to sleep in, surrounded by friends and some good home cooking from Auntie is enough to warm anyone's heart. But every day that passes, not even for a moment does my mind give in to any other thought, but Petra. I'm missing her morning moods; the house even feels emptier now.

Christa had done a great job with the dogs over the past few weeks. I found myself spending more and more time with them; I guess that was because they would just sit and listen to me babble on without judgment or questions. I found this very therapeutic to be honest.

It was in our interest to keep up with all the news from occupied Europe. The Germans had now developed and were using a new wonder weapon, the V1 buzzbomb. This new weapon was so called by the British because of the buzz noise its jet engine would make as it flew overhead. It was causing so much damage and is, by far, one of the most feared weapons the Germans had developed to date.

London was ablaze, as were other towns and cities across the southern coast of Britian. It is said that Hitler was hoping this new weapon would weaken the Allied spirit. It was causing so much destruction and many lives have been lost, but it had little effect on the Allied resolve.

It's now 13th June and a week since the D-day landings in Normandy. Still no sign of Petra and I am starting to lose all hope. I find myself drifting in my mind, searching for those images of us all, laughing, patching each other up, anything to keep her memory alive. I have considered that she has joined the thousands of lives already taken in this war. I am in no way a religious person but I can't help but think that Heidi is taking good care of her.

The Allies have now liberated 'Carentan' resulting in a firm beachhead for the Allied forces. This isn't going to be an easy task they have undertaken. At this rate it will take several months to finally overthrow the Reich machine.

More news from the papers and the radio, so far the Allies have landed well over three-hundred thousand troops, fifty thousand vehicles and one hundred tonnes of supplies into Normandy. This is no small feat, and it seems they are determined to succeed.

Before I know it, the end of June is upon us, and as the weeks have gone by, the sling has finally come off; my shoulder is quite stiff so I am trying to move it as much as possible. The news from France and the Allied advances are coming in thick and fast. They have now liberated inland as far as Caen. Cherbourg fell to US troops on the 27th.

The days continue to turn into weeks, the weeks into months. We're now over halfway through July and the first US troops enter Brittany with General Patten at the helm.

I have resigned myself to the fact that Petra has either being captured or is dead. Even if she was captured, by now they will have worked out who she is and would have shot her anyway. I have also found myself for the first time somewhat lost; Not knowing what direction to go in over the next few months has never been an issue for me. Main objectives were always to kill as many Germans as possible and take what they had. Now, I have no idea where to go. The Allies are doing a great job disposing of the most horrible race of humans ever to grace our wonderful world. Our assets here in Switzerland are doing well and constantly bringing in a nice profit. The Hong Kong deal will soon dry up; as the British will not need that resource once they and the other Allied forces finish the job at hand.

The loss of Heidi hit me hard, but losing Petra on top of that has taken me into a pit of sorrow. This conflict has cost me so much. In fact, almost everyone close to me has now been taken. I have come to realise why auntie reacted the way she did after the death of Heidi. Although I know I am not alone, but I feel so empty inside. If this is what war does to a person, then I never want to go through this again. Strolling around the compound and looking into the eyes of all these young ladies who have lost everything and everyone, I find myself filled with sadness. My heart is racing, my stomach feels like it as a bag of crazed rats inside, itching to get out. It takes all my inner strength to regain my posture.

There has been so much death in my life, yes, I have taken so many lives now, but in my mind, every single one of them deserved what they got. But now, I also find myself thinking about those who have been affected by my/our actions. Loss after all, is loss, and it doesn't matter which side you're on, those who are left behind, will be hurting. As the days went by, I found my sorrow turning to anger. Which meant I wasn't the nicest person to be around. I decided to turn my anger towards the only person in my world that was left, who was living on borrowed time. It was time to dedicate the next few weeks to finally organising the demise of Otto. Besides, we hadn't heard anything from London in weeks.

I made my mind up to send a couple of the girls back to the island to watch and report back to me on his movements. Within a couple of days, they are on their way. They hadn't had any chance to use any of their training yet, so this was a good starting point for them.

July 1944, it would seem that some of the top-ranking German officers have had enough of Hitler. On the 20th July they conspired to kill him, and almost succeeded. He was holding a secret war meeting at the Wolf's Lair in eastern Prussia. One of his top generals had placed a timed bomb under the table. It exploded but Hitler survived with minor injuries. You would think by now after all the killing they have done; they could kill one man.

However, the same could not be said for the conspirators and anyone remotely linked to it. Stauffenberg and one hundred and ninety-nine other officers were swifty rounded up and shot or hung. Others that were also involved directly - or even remotely suspected - of being involve in the attempted coup in Berlin on the same day of the bombing were also rounded up and shot. That totalled in over five thousand German soldiers taken from this world by their own side. What great news! Even the Nazis are killing off their own, now.

We're coming up on August and by the end of the month the German forces in Normandy and Brittany are now almost non-existent. In Paris, the French resistance rises up and begins to eject the German occupiers. By the 25th, French and US troops helps the resistance to liberate Paris. East of Paris, German forces are pushed back over the river Seine and British and Allied troops continued moving north of the river.

The girls I sent to the island are continuing to send back good intelligence on Otto; soon, it will be time to make my move. We haven't heard anything from London. In all honesty, I wasn't expecting it either. They did tell me to contact them once I had recovered, but I guess I forgot, well, that's what I will tell them if they ask. Besides, I am quite sure they now have no need for us girls any more. The liberation of war-torn occupied Europe is well underway. And pretty soon, there won't be any Third Reich soldiers left to kill. Currently, I am more than happy to stay at home and keep up to date with the Allied advances. It seems there isn't a day that goes by without reading or listening to news about the Germans losing ground or soldiers surrendering in their masses.

My mind continues to occasionally drift off regarding our Petra. Is her lifeless body lying in some woodland, a hedgerow maybe or some ditch by a road? Is she being tortured by the Gestapo? I attempt to stop these thoughts taking over me by rejoicing daily with the constant victories by the Allies.

During the first week of September, the Allied forces had liberated Antwerp and Brussel and are pushing on toward the Siegfried Line. The Siegfried line was built, back in the 1930's, by Hitler, it was akin to a last line of defence. It stretched from Kleve on the border with the Netherlands right down to our border here in Switzerland, over four hundred miles. It comprised of fortifications, bunkers, barbed wire and tank traps along the western German border, considered Germany's major line of defence. I guess that concept was about to be tested for the first and I hope for the very last time.

The dogs started to bark and growl, their ears picked up, their gaze turned towards the main gate. Someone unknown to them, was on the grounds. I started to make my way to the front of the house from the rear garden. As I neared the front edge of the house, the dogs had stopped barking and I could hear auntie, Christa and Mila shrieking like loudly. Once I turned the corner, I understood why. It was Petra! Overwhelmed with relief and with tears of joy streaming down my cheeks, I ran the last few feet towards her and scooped her up in a bear hug. I couldn't stop the flood of tears; she surely could feel my heart pounding as I held her tight.

I hadn't noticed two major factors though. One, she was actually on crutches and, two, she had travelled with someone. Petra kept shouting for me to be gentle, to put her down, but my excitement had taken over.

After a long minuet or so, when I did let her down, thank God for auntie and Mila. Who were already standing on either side of her. As I stood back, and watch the others embrace Petra, I realised why; she had broken her leg and it was still weak from being immobilised for several weeks.

I hugged auntie and Mila, tears still streaming down my face. I then turned to thank the stranger who returned Petra to us, only to then realise it was Maria, 'The Limping Lady'. We all went into the kitchen and, in true form, auntie made coffee and cake while Petra regaled us with her story.

They were attacking a small convoy. Everything was going well until one of her team shot the driver of the lead vehicle. This resulted in him pushing down hard on the accelerator and swerving all over the road; heading straight for her. She tried to jump out the of way and thought she had until she felt the wheels run over her leg. This resulted in her breaking it. If she didn't get treatment and soon, it could have turned into something very serious. So, with the Allies landing in Normandy behind them, they hijacked a car and headed for Paris. The resistance fighters she was with knew Paris well and they also knew that the hospital there was her only chance. Paris at this point was still occupied by the Germans, which actually worked in Petra's favour, because she was German. The only other issue was how to explain her injury. So, once they arrived in the city, they made contact with the Paris underground, who came up with a plan. Early the next morning, when hardly anyone would be about, they faked a car accident and placed Petra at the centre of the scene. All Petra had to do was come up with a solid story as to how and why it happened.

Petra

"So, there I was, lying in a hospital bed, my leg in a sling and totally unable to move or use the fucking toilet. Bedpans aren't easy to use with one leg up in the air, I can tell you. I explained.

"Anyway, in August things started really moving. We all were constantly kept up-to-date on the progress of the Allies. Finally, Paris was liberated and my leg was well on the mend. They were actually talking about removing the plaster of Paris." At last, decent coffee, I was ready for this, taking a couple of well-deserved gulps. "It had been a little over eight weeks at this point. I couldn't get word to you because the retreating Germans had cut all the phone lines and I thought that all the local radio operators were now out in the field with the Jedburgh.

" In the late afternoon, they brought in some new arrivals, one of which took the empty bed next to me. She had been fighting with the resistance here in Paris. She had not been shot, she had a few cuts and bruises but the most noticeable issue was her left leg. Well, the bottom half of it, at least; it was missing."

At this point, I realised Hannah was holding my hand so tightly she was cutting off the blood.

"Hannah, I'm here, I'm OK. I fucking need that hand though," pulling it away and shaking the blood back in to it. Appreciating her concern and love, I gently stroke her hand, before continuing my story. "And that is how I met this beautiful lady over here," turning and placing my hand on her shoulder and giving it a gentle squeeze. "I had to spend the next few days trying to work out how to use these fucking crutches, which, by the way, really rub on the under arms. Maria, was waiting on the nurses who were finding her a replacement leg. We just spent days wandering around the ward and gardens and helping each other.

"During this time, she told me about this other female she had met whilst attacking a depot in the middle of France. It was the same day as the Allies landed at Normandy. It wasn't long before I realised, she was talking about you Hannah."

"Maria then showed me the piece of paper that you had given her with our address on it that very same morning. It was fate, or something. We decided then we would travel home together; The war was over for both of us and it wouldn't be long before the Allies had taken back full control of Europe.

"Anyway, it would take more than a few fucking Nazis to kill me, eh girls?" I went to take a long-awaited bath and a change of clothes.

Hannah

I showed Maria to her room and let her get cleaned up. An hour later she joined me in the kitchen and we decided to go for a stroll round the grounds. Over the next few days this became a daily routine; helping Petra regain strength in her leg, strolls around our grounds and the nearby forest with Maria and telling each other war stories. Suddenly Maria stops me.

Maria

"Hannah, I need to talk to you about something important." Placing her hand on my shoulder.

"Yes, Maria." I replied

"Well, Maria, isn't my real name. It's Victoria Hall, I'm an American OSS agent. I have for several years now, also worked for the British in occupied France. This is how I became one of Germany's "Most Wanted" and my picture posted in almost every town and city. You girls have opened your doors and life's to me and so, I thought it was best to come clean, as a mark of respect."

"I have to say, I am not surprised Maria, sorry, Victoria. I have always known you are a spy, we are all spies, please don't worry yourself." Hannah, responded whilst holding both my arms gently and looking me clean in the eyes.

I was so pleased to get that off my chest; It's better to start a friendship on the truth. These girls have carved out a really nice life for themselves. Staying here in Switzerland, with them, one can truly forget there is a war on and the scenery is breathtaking. These girls, yes, they are battle hardened, they can be truthless, but they care about others. If they didn't, then why have they taken all these girls in, provided a safe haven, a place to call home, for so many of them.

Hannah

After Victoria's revelations, I decided to share Heidi's story with her. It took an hour or so, but I could tell she really cared, listening intently and hugging me when she could see the emotions flooding in. Without hesitation, she asked if she could use her contacts in the US, to help me with the Otto situation, which I was pleased to graciously accept. She made a few calls once we returned home and it was now, a waiting game.

Over the past few months, I hadn't read all the newspapers. I decided it was time for a catch up on current events, so, I spent the rest of the day going through them.

It's November and the Allies have advanced some three hundred and fifty miles, but have stalled due to them not been prepared for such things, such as the almost complete collapse of the German army over the past few months. Other concerns were supply chain issues and so on. The Germans were also now fighting on two fronts, and on almost only German soil. They had the Allied forces on the western front and to the east they had to contend with the Soviet army, who are attacking without mercy. They are killing, raping and burning everything and everyone, they come across. The Red Army had advanced some four hundred and fifty miles in five weeks, taking their lead, I think, from the German blitzkrieg manoeuvre, but in a more ruthless fashion. At this rate, there will be nothing but rubble left of Germany by the end of this war.

Mid to Late November 1944

It has been reported that the German Army has been given a little breathing space, due to the Allied forces in the West sluggishness, and the Red Army's purposeful halting at Warsaw in Poland. This gave the German army time to regroup. Let us not forget Italy, the Germans are losing ground there too.

It surely will not be too long before the total collapse of the Third Reich.

Chapter Ten
December 1944

It's been a busy December for both the Allies and Germany - there have been major advances and counter attacks on both sides. Maria has settled in for the time being and it seems she still has some pull over in the US. The girls returned from the island to enjoy the festivities here with us.

Petra and I worked together to get her back to full fitness. We also discussed what direction we will go in once the war is over. Petra, much like myself, wants to continue with the status quo, but that's only great during wartime. It wouldn't work without the cover of a war, which provided us with some anonymity, but then we will have to make some changes to ensure success and not being chased down by any police, or any other major authority from different countries.

The situation is going to take time to work out but, for now, a more pressing issue needs our attention; Maria has informed me that she has a small gift for me. Apparently, it's coming by special courier and will be arriving today. Well, Christmas has come and gone, but I do enjoy a nice gift from time to time. With eager anticipation, I kept looking out the window until, finally, a lorry came up the driveway. What could this gift possibly be that it requires such large transportation vehicle, I wondered?

Four rather muscly men get out of the cabin and head for the back of the lorry. As I go out to take the delivery, I see a large wooden crate now sitting on the ground. Curious. My face must have looked so puzzled to the men as I walked towards them. The driver asked me to sign for the crate, which I did, and they drove off. As they did, Maria and Petra came out, with Maria holding a crowbar and a hammer.

"Here you go, Hannah," she says, with a quirk of her lips.

"What the fuck is this?" Petra asks.

"I have no idea but, according to the stamps on the box, it has come all the way from America," I replied, scratching my chin.

"Before you open this, Hannah, there is something I need to say," Maria says, placing one hand on top of the crate.

"Oh, come on, it's fucking freezing out here. Get on with it," grumbles Petra, with her arms folded across her chest whilst jumping up and down on the spot.

"Go on, Maria," I urged, because my nipples are so hard you could hang hats on them.

"This is a gift from me and my people over in the US. There is however, something attached to this gift." She says whilst pacing around the crate, and tapping the top. "If you accept and open it, then you and your girls will owe us a favour. Do you agree?" She pauses, waiting for an answer.

"A favour? what kind of favour?" I ask.

"Nothing too big, and certainly nothing outside of your skillset," she replies, her smile quickly turning into a knowing smirk.

For the last few years, we have been controlled by the British, which none of us liked. I have to consider this carefully, the last thing we needed now is having to work under another government. The situation needed to be clarified.

"Maria, this favour, is it a one-off job and that's it? I asked.

"Yes, Hannah, one job and we are even.

"Ok, I agree," nodding my head, staring Maria straight in the eye and shaking her hand.

After a lot of tugging, groaning and a few choice cuss words coming from my own mouth, I finally managed to pry open the crate. Standing at one end of the crate and Petra on the other, we dug the ends of our crowbars beneath the lip and pried the lid off and peered inside.

"Holy fucking, shit, Hannah!" Petra, screams.

I stood there, completely still while I looked down into the crate, eyes wide and my jaw growing slack. Is that...? I looked up to find Maria nodding, her smile only growing wider. I stepped back; I needed a moment to collect myself.

Inside the crate was a body. An adult, male body.

"What kind of gift is this, Maria? Is this a nasty joke or something? I asked.

Maria, laughed and shaking her head replies "No."

"He is still alive, but heavily sedated. Now, you might want to take a proper look at his face, Hannah," Maria insisted.

Petra was straight in there, grabbing a fistful of his hair and lifting his head high and turned his face towards me.

My legs gave way from under me when I saw him, one hand rising to cover my mouth. Feeling my body shake, I hadn't realised I had started crying until I blinked, the world around me quickly becoming blurry.

"Otto."

I looked at Petra and, without saying a word, she turned his head around and took a good look. A second later, she threw his head against the side of the crate with some considerable force and yells,

"Finally, got you, mother fucker!"

"Petra, this isn't your gift, don't damage him, well, not too much, not yet," I roar at her.

"Let's get some of the others and get him inside," I asked Petra.

Within a short time, Otto was down in our cellar, locked up and secured to a large metal table. Once that was done, I had to take a moment and went back up to the kitchen and had a stiff drink and a smoke. Now, all we had to do, was devise some truly horrific way to end this man, and it wasn't going to be quick.

Petra was already suggesting a few ideas. Peeling his skin off. Taking a hammer to his hands and feet.

Pushing a stick of dynamite up his rectum and lighting it. With each new idea voiced, it was clear Petra was becoming more and more excited by the idea of Otto's demise. Unexpectedly, even auntie was chipping in with ideas. Chop his testicles off, cook them and feed them to him. Put some rats in there with him, cut him, and let them eat him alive.

Petra hadn't killed anyone in a few weeks so she was understandably getting a little bit itchy. In honour of our Heidi, though, I had to bide my time with Otto. Besides, nothing else was happening in our little world right now, and it would do Otto some good to anticipate his punishment.

We have four days to go until the new year, so I decided to leave him to his thoughts, the girls took it in turns to feed and water him, I wanted him at full strength before we started.

All the girls help auntie in prepare food for the new year, making something taught to them by their mothers and that was traditionally eaten at this time of year. I couldn't tell you what some of it was, but it smelled nice. Christa had even made little festive hats for the dogs, which they spent most of the time pushing off.

Auntie and some of the other girls had made a great job of decorating the dining room for the festive period, although we did have to bring over some extra tables and chairs from the annexe to fit everyone in..

Our family is growing; there are fifty of us now, and we even have a couple of girls from the Asian theatre of war. These girls are already considered masters in the martial arts, though, so it seems like training next year is going to become far more intense.

January 1945

It's a new year and I, for one, am hoping the rest of the girls are waking up feeling the same as I am: Hungover! Nevertheless, there is work to be done. Christa has been visiting our guest in the cellar with the boys to ensure two things; Firstly, that they had his scent and secondly, to make Otto aware that, if he tried to escape, they would be coming for him.

He has started pleading for food and water, I have been informed, and that's exactly how I wanted him. I am going to take a few hours to get through this headache, first, though, and try to eat something before we start.

After breakfast, I collected a few things from the work shed before Petra and I headed down to the cellar. Some of the other girls expressed that they wanted to come and watch but this, to us, was personal. Besides, I had a small task for a few of them to complete over the next couple of days.

After unlocking the cellar door, I walked in and placed some items on a small table in the corner, well within otto's line of sight. The smell in the room wasn't very pleasant; human excrement and un-washed body odour filled the room. As the pong hit my senses my eyes started running, I could feel chunks of my breakfast in the back of my throat, fighting to escape. It's intensity is so strong I had to place my hand over my mouth and nose and force a swallow to keep everything in.

Over the past few years, we have learned a lot about the human body, be it male or female. Their wants and needs, their desires and, more importantly, how much pain it can tolerate. It is really quite astounding that, by using the correct methods and good timing, you can torture someone for weeks if you need to.

Depriving the body of water for several days, for example, can result in the inability to speak. I wanted this man to be able to use his vocal cords, so the first thing I did was to give him a drink. Then with Petra holding down his right hand, I took the pliers and, starting with his little finger, squeezing the jaws tightly on his fingertip. As I gripped his finger, he started to moan, low and deep in his throat, shaking his head, weakly and begging me not to do it, Otto started to shuffle about in a feeble attempt to free himself, but to no end; he is well tied down. With plenty of force focused on his finger, I slowly start to lift the pliers upwards.

First came the snap; the sound of bone cracking against the quiet of the room as his finger broke at the knuckle. The swelling that followed was almost immediate.

One down, nine to go.

His whole body had started to shake uncontrollably. It becoming hard to distinguish the tears from the bullets of sweat now rolling down his face. As I worked my way towards his thumb, his muffled screams started to grow higher, each desperate sound managing to seep through the gag over the crunch of each bone.

When our friend Daphne killed her husband, she had used a makeshift hammer and nails to aid her in his demise. I'm going to borrow that idea, but, with a twist; Taking five nails, I bound them together, turned them down on their heads and, with a hammer, proceeded to blunt them; this gave the nails a nice, split-type edge, perfect for what I have in mind for Otto.

I took three and, grazing the point of the nail over his left hand, ensured each one hovered over a bone. Ignoring his groans of protest, I raised my hammer high and swiftly brought it down. Otto screamed against the gag, his body jolting upwards. Once I had started, though, I couldn't stop; a cold desire to hear each splintered crack of his bones coursed through my body, his garbled moans quickening the speed in which I punctured his flesh. I was not satisfied until the dull *clang* of metal against metal rang above the strangled cries, his hand swollen and bloodied while it twitched against the table it was now pinned down to. His hand is definitely broken now and, hopefully, some of the bones will be splintered, too.

At this point, I was aware that I had set Petra's inner demon aflame; she had been pleading with me to let her have a go, a wicked smile on her lips. Looking over my work, I supposed it would be nice to share. So, putting down the hammer, I stepped back with a nod and allowed Petra to have her turn

Taking hold of the pliers, Petra gleefully began the meticulous task of pulling each fingernail from his left hand. With one finger pulled taut, Petra began to carefully extract his nail. Otto's hand strained against the nail packs while she worked and, biting down on his saliva-soaked gag, screamed pitifully against the fabric while Petra hummed over his pathetic cries.

I couldn't help but smile at her choice; by combining the nail packs and methodically removing his fingernails, Petra would effectively double this bastard's pain and further her own fun in torturing him.

At this time, I needed a smoke. We decided we would have a coffee and, when we got to the kitchen we found auntie, who asked how it was going. As auntie and I talked, I could feel Petra getting increasingly twitchy beside me; she wanted to know what we would be doing next, and which body part would be our focus.

I told Petra this would be a good place to stop for the day. She isn't exactly known for her patience and, while she was happy to keep going, I took a moment to discuss the finer points of waiting and not taking anything too far too soon. Obviously, Petra wasn't happy with this but, after hearing my side, she agreed to stop for the day.

Only once we had added one final element to Otto's session today, that is.

Taking several buckets of warm water down to the basement with us, we washed both Otto and the room down a little. Then, just before leaving him for the night, Petra began pouring large quantities of salt over his open wounds, making sure she didn't miss any. The use of the warm water would help the salt to dissolve into his open wounds, serving two purposes; one, it cleaned them all out but, more importantly,

"It stings like fuck," Petra had stated gleefully during our break.

Standing in the open doorway, we watched the bastard writhe and try to scream. Smiling down at him, we waved goodbye, but not without a final "See you tomorrow, motherfucker," from Petra before I shut and locked the door.

Day two.

Now, if you want to cause pain and suffering without causing major injury, it's best to start with the small bones, places that the body doesn't really need in order to keep functioning. That means, hands, feet, and, yes, teeth. If you have ever had a tooth pulled, you know it hurts, but normally the dentist will provide with some kind of pain relief to tolerate it.

Taking a long, thin leather strap, we removed Otto's gag and placed the band into his mouth, over his lower jaw and tied it under and around the table. Once that was secure, Petra jumped up on the table and, grabbing his hair, pulled Otto's head back so that his mouth stayed open, thus providing easy access to his upper teeth.

Without the gag to keep him quiet, Otto started pleading for us to stop. Taking no notice of him, I took a pair of pliers from the table and pulled the first three teeth. Each *pop* and *crack* of a tooth separating from his jaw filled my ears, even over the garbled screams

I probably got a little carried away; Petra had to remind me that we had agreed to take it in turns to pull a tooth. Handing Petra the pliers, I stepped back and let her get to work.

We didn't want to rush this, so it took us several hours to pull the top set of his teeth out. Just before we were ready to return the gag, however, Otto started mumbling something. It was difficult to understand, at first; perhaps it was the mouthful of blood.

He gargled a second and third time. It sounded like someone trying to sing whilst drinking water.

"It's here. You can have it if you let me go," he finally managed to say on the fourth try.

"What's here?" I asked.

"The money," he babbled, his bloodshot eyes trained on me. "The money is here, in a numbered account. It's here and you can have it all, if you let me go," he repeated, blood and spittle dripping from his mouth with every word.

Petra and I left the room for a short moment to discuss this new revelation from Otto. We decided to ignore this for the moment but make a mental note of it for future reference.

At this point, it was time to break for the day, but not before we played with Otto's head a little more. We proceeded to clean and bandage his right hand, which had become fully swollen to the wrist. While I went to retrieve the bandage, Petra took her time to cross his fingers, one over the other to ensure even more discomfort. Once she was done, I tightly wound the bandage over his digits.

Then we started on his left hand, pulling the nails out before adding more salt water, ignoring the pathetic sobs that escaped his mouth. Once we were finished, we bandaged that hand up, too. I gave him one last drink of water – his voice needed to be ready for tomorrow – replaced his gag and checked that all the knots would hold for the night. We then had a quick clean-up of the room and left for the day.

We locked the door and headed up to the kitchen. By this point, it was dinner time and many of the girls from the annex had gathered in the main house. Unsurprisingly, they were eager to see what we had done to him and, after a quick discussion with Petra and auntie, we agreed that the girls should take a look.

"It will make or break them," Auntie said, before taking them three at a time to the cellar.

Whilst the remaining girls excitedly waited by the cellar door, Petra and I discussed the money Otto had mentioned.

We agreed that this wasn't about the money, but about honouring our word to Heidi. Of course, you can never have too much money. It would certainly provide a stronger foundation and enable us to help more girls and, while we are unsure of how much is actually left, the man had bought an island; who knows what else he has purchased outside of the extensive building work he added to his floating pile of dirt.

We agreed to sleep on it; over-night. One thing is for sure, though; we'll never let him go, no matter how much he is willing to pay.

Day three.

While I was sat having my morning coffee when one of the girls that I had sent on a job walked in.

"Successful?" I asked.

"Yes, Hannah. Where would you like them?" she replied.

"Separate and lock them in different rooms in the cellar." I instructed her.

Petra entered the kitchen, she just nodded in my direction and sat at the table with a coffee.

"Our guests have arrived," I informed her and, leaving her to wake up, decided to go for a morning stroll around the gardens

Upon my return, Petra had come round and was ready for the day ahead, but not before continuing our discussion regarding the money.

"We shall take what we can from him," I explained. "It isn't like he is going to need it, anyway."

Petra and I made our way down to him and, after releasing his gag, asked for his bank and account number. He seemed almost relieved and did this without question. Next, I asked him how much was left; it turns out you can buy quite a lot with a few million, and he still had nearly twenty-five million of it left. Now, it will be put to good use.

I had instructed two of the other girls to stay in the cellar while Petra and I talked to Otto. During this time, they were to bring our guests out and tie them to separate chairs while facing the door to his room. Since their extraction, they have both been blindfolded and gagged and have no idea where they are or who has taken them

Causing pain and suffering to a human body is easy and, depending on the injury, the body will, given time, fix itself. If both the body and mind are affected together, however, the lasting anguish it can cause is often irreparable. For certain individuals, this form of punishment is far more fitting.

Today we introduce him to his first and last taste of mental torture.

Climbing onto the table from behind, Petra gripped his hair and wrenched Otto's head up again. He groaned pitifully; he must have thought it was time to remove the rest of his teeth. Instead of reaching for the pliers, however, I moved towards the door and watched his face contort in pained confusion.

Swinging the door open, Petra and I's smiles only grew when he finally saw what lay beyond it. There, staring back at him from the open doorway sat his wife and son, their blindfolds since removed.

Tears stained their faces while they writhed in their chairs, straining against the binds while muffled screams and jumbled words strained against their gags. It took a moment but, slowly, realisation dawned on Otto's face and, as anticipated, he lost it.

He fought against his restraints, pulling and screaming in a bid to be near his family. Petra fought to pull him back, pulling against the chains as if they were the reins on a horse. Turning back to the girls, I gestured to one of them to return the boy to his room; the young one shouldn't be witness to this, but it was time for Otto to understand what it felt like to have a loved one taken from you

I walked over to his wife with a knife, still mottled with her husband's blood. Slowly, I started to stroke the blade down her cheek and along the ridges of her lovely throat while she shuddered beneath its touch.

"Hannah, wait," Petra calls. I look over at her, the blade of my knife pressing into the wife's skin. "He's trying to say something."

I remove Otto's gag, blood and snot shower the table whilst he clears his throat, through the spluttering and coughing we could just make out what he was trying to say.

"In the same bank there is a strong box. It's filled with gold and jewels. If you allow them both to live and don't hurt them, I will tell you where to find the key," he pleads, his voice hoarse and words slurring. I watch as the tears start to pool in his eyes and begin to slip down his bloodied cheeks.

Petra sighs dramatically and, stuffing the gag back into Otto's mouth, turns to look at me.

"Fuck that, we don't need any more money. Just kill the bitch."

I don't need to be told twice. Moving discreetly to one side, I pull out my pistol and, in one careful movement, aimed the barrel at the woman's head and *squeezed*.

The *crack* of the gun rattled against the cellar walls, the echo of a high-pitched scream quickly following suit. Letting me arm fall, the pistol heavy against my leg, I turned away from the mess beside me and looked toward the table where Otto wailed.

Petra and I laughed, watching while he slammed his head against the metal surface, crushing his nose into a bloodied mess.

Once he had tired himself out, I walked over and patted him on the head. "There, there," I said, my voice low. "You shot Heidi, so I shot your wife."

I closed the door and we started on his lower jaw.

Despite the physical pain he was going through, he is now wondering what we're going to do to his son. Taking a life is part of who we are and what we do, but taking the life of a child is something that goes against everything we stand for. Of course, he doesn't know that.

The Reich have caused so much pain and suffering over the past few years, indiscriminately killing anyone who they thought inferior to their race; this included torturing and killing children. This he knows and so, in his mind, if they can do that, then so can others.

Day four.

The room was becoming a little ripe, so we took some more buckets of water down to the cellar to give it a wash. Once we were done, we turned our attention back to Otto. Today, we have devised something special for him.

Although he is still firmly chained to the table, there is still room for a little movement. For his punishment today, we need to prevent him from being able to move his feet, so Petra and I took some straps and secured his ankles to the table, ensuring he had no movement.

Levelling my gaze with Otto's, I reached into my pocket and brought out a packet of smokes and lit the first cigarette. Then I lit another, and another, with Petra following suit and lighting her own.

We proceeded to stub each one out onto the soles of his feet. Pathetic whimpers and the smell of burnt skin started to fill the room while we re-lit the longer cigarettes; we don't like waste, after all.

There were a few times where he passed out, meaning we had to stop our task and bring him back around. Petra took great delight in slapping him around the face to rouse him; we didn't want him to miss a moment of this game, after all.

He is starting to pass out a lot more, now. I don't think he can take much more of this. Taking a look at his feet, I was satisfied to see that both soles were now covered in angry, red marks and weeping blisters. Satisfied with our work, Petra and I decided to leave him alone for the rest of the day

Day five.

We had packed Otto's nuts in ice the night before, periodically going down to the cellar to replace it before it could melt. Though this might seem like a less painful method, there was a reason for this brand of torture.

After finishing our coffee and breakfast, Petra and I headed down to his room to see how he was doing.

He is alive, just. I am not sure how much more he can actually take.

Scraping back what was left of the ice, I handed Petra a knife and took out my own. Then, each taking a turn, we proceeded to slice open his nuts and remove them for him. The bastard passed out immediately from the contact of the blade; there wasn't even a moan or a whine coming past his lips. Once we were done, we placed his balls on top of the table.

Bringing him round again, the first thing Otto could see were his testicles in front of him. Realisation slowly dawned and, soon after, the pain of the extraction hit him. He didn't react, though; there were no words spoken, no movement made. He had given up. I could see it in his eyes.

There's still more to do, of course; shooting him would be an act of mercy, I believe, so that's out of the question. Instead, I nodded to Petra and, taking our knives, we proceeded to insert the bloodied blades into his body, making sure to take our time with each insertion.

I could feel the blade scrape against the bone, the sound scratching against my ears. A couple of times I had to push down with more force, especially when the blade seemed to hit bodily obstructions. We continued our task, slowly moving up and down, up and down his torso, his skin a pattern of cuts and scars.

He died with a final, strangled moan while we sliced open his gut. As a final act, though, Petra extracted her blade from his body and, moving lower down the table, proceeded to cut off his manhood.

Holding the flaccid member tight in her hand, I watched as Petra pushed it into his mouth, a cruel smile twisting on her lips while she stared down at his lifeless corpse.

"*Tschüss*, Cock sucker!"

Chapter Eleven

Hannah

We went to sleep that evening with a feeling of self-satisfaction. Finally, we had avenged our sister and we can now close that chapter of our lives. Well, almost; there's just a couple of things to take care of. We have to get rid of the body and also return his son to Britain.

The two girls that brought Otto's family over requested they return his son. They also asked us something that was niggling me: How does a German Gestapo Officer marry and have a child with an English woman?

Mila had the answer and proceeded to explain, "It was quite simple, really. Back in the early 1930's, he was educated in England and that was where he met and married her. They lived in Britain until war broke out, where he returned to Germany to serve his country. A good woman and loyal son were clearly less to him than his beloved Führer and Germany."

Otto's son is fourteen years old and, knowing his parents had been taken from him, we had to ensure he didn't want revenge at a later date. So, prior to leaving with him, the girls took him to see what we had done to his father and mother. His response was quite shocking, actually; he didn't speak a word or shed a tear. Instead, his expression remained neutral.

It can be assumed that, for the first eight years of his life, he was brought up on a strict Hitlerite diet.

Having a high-ranking German officer for a father, he most certainly would have joined the Hitler youth. Although not mandatory until 1936, it was expected by Hitler that all German officer's sons joined the organisation from the age of six years old. That's more than enough years to fill his head with propaganda and turn him into a cold-hearted human. I have no doubt that, being English, Otto's wife struggled with this in more ways than one. The final straw would have been their son reaching his tenth birthday.

Once ten years old, all boys would undergo a diligent investigation regarding their racial purity. He would have been exposed as half English/German, and Mother and son would have been taken to a camp. Or worse, shot. Hence them fleeing back to England.

The two girls informed Otto's son that what happened to his parents could also happen to him. Fear is a great motivator to keep him from seeking revenge. Besides, he had no idea who we were or where he was, but that has not stopped even the most determined person from looking.

Once certain the boy understood his own mortality, the girls returned him back to what is left of his family in England the same day.

Now, to remove the body; we thought it would be fitting to return Otto back to his beloved country. With this in mind, we got hold of a Gestapo uniform, dressed him in it, smuggled him over the border where a waiting car was fuelled and ready to go. We drove to a nearby small grass airfield; one we have used before. The gent that owns the field and plane is considered a good friend. It helps that we pay very well, too.

The plane had German markings but was not fitted with any guns, mostly used as a reconnaissance plane. It could fly over Germany without any issues from the ground, and the allies don't shoot down unarmed planes. Petra went with Otto and, once over Germany, she sent him on his way, pushing him out of the plane with a note pinned to his chest:

"Tod der gesamten Gestapo" (Death to all Gestapo)

Over the next couple of days, Petra and I felt rather pleased with ourselves, but it would seem that today was the day we would have to repay our debt to the people that gave us this opportunity in the first place.

A car we didn't recognise drove up the driveway. Maria must have known they were coming as, by the time we went outside, she was already there to meet them. We will have to discuss this at a later date; if she wants to continue living with us, she will need to learn to communicate.

They spoke for a short time before she brought them over to meet me at the door. From their style of dress, I could tell they are American. After they introduced themselves as Mr Brown and Mr Smith, I invited them in for a coffee and we headed for the kitchen where Petra and auntie were sat at the table having a chat.

For almost an hour they regaled us with war stories from the Pacific theatre. It would seem that the Japanese are a formidable, head strong force.

"That is all very nice, but what the fuck does that have to do with us?" Petra asks tartly.

"Nothing at all," Mr Brown replies. "We thought it would be nice to get to know each other. After all, we going to be working together."

This was going nowhere and, quite frankly, both Petra and I were becoming annoyed. I noticed Petra glaring at Mr Brown; I can't blame her; he was quite irritating.

"We are not big on small talk, so cut the crap and tells us what you need us to do," I ask.

"It would seem that three of our agents have been compromised," Mr Brown says, standing up to light another cigarette. "We now believe them to be double agents. Not for the Germans, but for the Soviets."

He continues briefing us while he walks around the kitchen. He then nodded towards Mr Smith, who picks up his leather briefcase, flips it open and pulls out a file. They have everything on these three individuals apart from who their contacts are.

"As they are American citizens, we cannot take them out ourselves. So, we need you to firstly fill in the blanks and then kill them." Mr Smith specified.

"Ummm, you bring us one and you want three in return? There is something not quite right with those numbers," I replied.

"Well, we do bring an added incentive." Mr Smith stated, putting his hand inside his briefcase once more. Pulling a clenched fist out, he set his bag on the floor and placed his palm upon the tabletop.

"As we understand it, you might be interested in this?" Mr Brown gestured to Mr Smith to open his hand.

Petra's eyes lit up as she, like me, realised what we are looking at: The lock box key that Otto had been talking about the other day.

"You clearly know what this is," Mr Smith began, watching us both with keen interest. "And what is in the box this key opens. By now I am sure you have cleaned out his bank account; this would be the icing on the cake for you girls, I should say."

I excused myself for a moment whilst I went and found Mila. Since her arrival, she has grown a large network of people, with her reach extending into Asia and the US. They are all very willing to pass on information; for a small fee, of course.

She is doing a great job, filling Heidi's shoes.

Upon returning to the kitchen with Mila, I asked Mr Smith if he would leave the file, they had brought with them and allow us a couple of days to digest it. My request was granted, and so they left with a promise they would return in a couple of days. Maria arranged to meet them for dinner later that evening at their hotel.

Petra and I spent a few hours going over the information together. One issue that has come to our attention is that, of these three agents, one already resides here in Switzerland.

Although we had just spent the last few days torturing Otto in our own home, it had been an unwritten rule before this that we would never bring work into our sanctuary. As Petra reminded me recently: "Never shit where you eat."

If we're going to take this contract, then we will need a plan to get this target out of the country or, at the very least, ensure we will not be seen. Another issue is, these are US citizens; yes, the contract comes from a US department, but this could cause us some serious issues later on.

We left it alone for the rest of the day to provide Mila time to do her thing. Besides, we needed confirmation on these targets whereabouts and current places they visit regularly.

I went off with my trusty sketch pad for some well-deserved me time. I don't know what Petra was going to do in her spare time; in fact, I don't think I have recently asked her what she gets up to these days. It seems, for the past year or so, I have become somewhat introverted, self-consumed. As long as no one is in any danger, then I am not interested or so it has now come to my attention, this may well be the case. I will have to work on this.

The next morning after coffee and a small bite to eat, Petra and I went to see Mila for an update.

"It is confirmed; all three are where they are supposed to be, ladies," she confirmed as we walked in the room. This room is now packed out with filing cabinets, each drawer clearly marked. There is even one for all our girls, filled with detailed information on all our strengths and weaknesses.

Another drawer, which used to be one of Heidi's favourites, is the one marked '*Allies / Informants*'. This speaks for its self; anyone we deal with or is on the pay role, basically.

Possible future targets is another one. This drawer may have to be revisited once this war is over, only because it's full of German targets only at this time. Then there are several others with even more information on various individuals, countries... you name it, she has a drawer for it. Incredible, really.

It suddenly occurred to me though, if we allow Mila to go out and work in the field as we did Heidi, then it's highly possible we could lose her, too.

Back to the issue at hand. Mila continued to brief us on everything else she had found out regarding these individuals. Then we all went up to the kitchen to try and formulate some kind of plan for each one.

1. How to draw them in.
2. Method.
3. Place.
4. Time of day.

It was decided by all that this could be done to a satisfactory conclusion but would take a few days to complete. We had to gather more information to ensure we didn't get caught or seen by anyone.

We also agreed that we couldn't use our normal poison method as the British and the Americans would immediately know it was us. With this in mind, we had to come up with another killing method aside from that.

Knives are messy, but when used correctly can prove effective. Silenced pistols, despite their name, are anything but; if someone is close enough they can still be heard. An explosive accident could work, but that's not exactly quiet. It could also result in others been injured or killed, depending on the location and its proximity to other buildings.

Over the next few hours, we went through many other methods aside from these. Before we knew it, Mr Brown and Mr Smith had returned.

They enter the kitchen and we made coffee whilst they settled in.

"We have looked over this and yes, we will do this for you," I informed them, watching their reaction to our answer. "However, we might need some help with certain specialist equipment."

"And what equipment will you need?" asks Mr Brown.

"Not sure yet," I reply, turning to look at Petra, who is glaring at both men. "We will need a few days to prepare each target properly. We are having each target followed by our people as we speak."

"Then it is agreed. You let Maria know what you need and when, and we will do our best to get that for you." Replies Mr Brown.

"Maria had told us that you are very capable girls," Mr Smith added, looking first at me and then Petra. "We look forward to the completion of this issue and, who knows, we may even work together again in the future. Depending on the success of this mission, of course." Mr Smith added.

Government people do enjoy their control over people and their objectives. Even my tolerance of this is becoming thin, glancing over at Petra, I could tell by the expression on her face, she just wanted to shoot them both. Then, if someone was scrutinising my every curve with the intensity they are towards Petra, that would make my blood boil.

"We will see. We're not sure which way we are going right now," I explain, watching Petra from the corner of my eye. She only seems to become angrier the longer we sit here. "We might even make this our last mission. After all, some of us have seen enough death to last two life times."

At this declaration, Mr brown and Mr smith exchanged looks of disapproval before turning back to us both.

"That would be a sad day. You ladies are so talented," Mr Smith sighed, tapping his fingers on top of the table. "It would be a shame to waste it and all that training you have gone through." Replied Mr Smith.

At this, Petra piped up. "You guys would do well to remember that flattery does not fucking work on us."

"Would you mind not using that language with us, Petra," Mr. Brown says, his gaze turning stern when he looked towards Petra.

There was a short moment of silence, but I could feel it in the air and see in Petra's eyes she was about to go off. It was like watching a volcano about to erupt and oh boy, did she.

"Listen, shit head," Petra snarled, rising from her chair until she was looking down on both men. "You're in our home and here, we can be exactly who we are." Kicking her chair back, Petra paced the length of the kitchen, her eyes not once leaving the men sat at the table. "I am sick to death of been told what to do and say by so called men of power. If you don't like it, then just fuck off!" She angrily shouts.

With a final wave of her middle finger, Petra turned on her heels and stalked out of the kitchen, slamming the door behind her to leave a deafening silence.

The men just sat there, totally stunned and a little red faced.

"Somewhat hot headed that one, isn't she?" Mr Brown comments after a few seconds.

"She hasn't even got started yet, I think it's time for you both to leave."

They both stand up and put their coats and hats on, said their goodbyes and Maria walked them out. Auntie was giggling to herself and I have to admit, I had a little smile on my face too.

Petra walked back in to the kitchen a few minutes later and again had a few more choice words about our new OSS friends. Maria returned and caught the back end of her comments. Although she didn't directly defend them, they are her bosses and it is her agency Petra is attacking.

It was decided to move forward with the closest target first, which meant a trip to Zurich. Petra and I packed a bag and set off to the train station; we could have drove, but the train journey would allow more time to consider and formulate the finer points of the plan.

Upon arrival, we booked ourselves into the same hotel he was staying at. He was posing as an American business man, here to negotiate on the export of silk cloth from Basel. However, the actual reason he was here was to procure weapons. For many years now, the Swiss have produced and sold weapons to many countries across Europe, including Germany.

American cargo ships are hunted by German U-Boats constantly as they cross the Atlantic Ocean. As a back-up and to fill any gaps, it was thought that, for a continuous supply of these essential items to the British and their own troops, the Swiss were their best bet. Our target hasn't been sticking to his objective; for whatever reason, he had been compromised and has instead been providing the Soviets with detailed information, such as lists of contacts, weapon availability, agent names and locations.

It wasn't too long before we had made contact with the double agent.

Petra and I met up with one of our local contacts and he filled us in with the latest updates on the targets current movements. He never seemed to go anywhere that wasn't highly populated. Petra eventually went back to continue surveillance whilst our contact took me to find a secluded barn or house that we could lure the target into just outside the city.

Soon enough we found the perfect spot. A barn surrounded by nothing but fields, the perfect place for a kill zone. We returned back to our hotel and Petra and I sat down for our evening meal.

We are just enjoying our second glass of wine when Petra's face warped into a state of confusion. Then she started gesturing for someone to come over and I finally turned around to see who she was looking at.

I couldn't believe my eyes; it was Christa! She approached our table and sat down and, after the basic *"how do you do's,"* she started to explain why she was here.

In short, she wanted more field experience and thought the quickest way to learn was with us. Petra and I had to agree; Christa would draw the target in. It was a perfect plan, and Christa was proving herself to be a great asset to us all.

There was no denying that she was a delight to behold; Christa was a beauty by anyone's standards. Standing at 5"6 with light blue eyes and blonde hair, a slim but curvy figure, Christa was the picture of every man's fantasy. This fact had been confirmed earlier when she joined us, as most of the men in the room had been fixated on her every step. Every man including our target.

We sit chatting for a few minutes, I take a cigarette and several of the gentlemen close by rush to provide me with a light, finishing my smoke, we leave and head for bed.

The next morning, I went down for breakfast first and, five minutes later, wearing the tightest dress she could find and showing just enough skin, Christa soon followed and made a point of passing our targets table. Seating herself close enough to him, she made sure to look and smile in his direction.

It took almost thirty minutes of shy glances and nervous smiles from Christa before he approached her. Immediately, he made his intentions quite clear; he wanted to be in her company, at least for that evening.

Petra arrived shortly after this exchange, joining me at my table directly behind the target. While sipping our coffees, we caught some of their conversation. First, he asked about us; Christa told him that we had been friends for many years before informing him that she was actually here with her parents for a couple of days.

"And where are they now?" he asked her.

"Out visiting family," she replied. "That is why my friends are here; to keep an eye me. But, as we grew up together, they know that all women have needs."

He became curious then, and Christa explained that her father was a very strict person who did not approve of any kind of pre-marital encounters. We then watched as she slowly leaned over to gently caress his hand and, in a low voice, said,

"However, I am somewhat of a rebel." She fluttered her eyelashes and smiled coquettishly, stroking her finger over his knuckles. "I don't like to follow my father's instructions."

"We have to be careful," she whispered. "If we're going to do this, it needs to be somewhere out of the way; my friends can only cover for me for so long in the hotel. We must go out of the city for a few hours, just you and me."

The idea of a covert liaison with a beauty such as Christa seemed to excite the man, and he took very little convincing to join her for a secret rendezvous. I had to pinch Petra to stop her from saying something unsavoury; yes, he was a typical man, but we could not let him think we were against this in any way. In his mind, we were aiding Christa in her rebellious pursuits.

Before they left, the target gave Christa his room number and asks her to leave him a time and address at the front desk later that day. Christa enthusiastically obliged and, standing from the table, was ready to take her leave, but not before the man had kissed her hand and bid his goodbyes.

Once he had left, Petra and I nodded in Christa's direction while taking another sip of coffee, silently congratulating her on a job well done. The trap was set.

Later that day, our contact drove us out to the barn. Christa had also driven there earlier in one of our own vehicles, except she wasn't alone; she had brought the boys with her, and this would act as their first test.

We knew where Christa would be waiting, so Petra and I went to the surveillance point in the barn that I had chosen for us the day before. It did not take long for our target to arrive, or for him to engage with Christa the moment he locked eyes on her.

With eager anticipation, his demeanour changed and he pulled her into a tight embrace. His eyes had grown dark and his breath became heavy while his hands roamed lower down her back. Christa tried to pull away, telling him to wait, but he didn't listen; an animal had been unleashed.

Gripping her backside, the target refused to let go despite Christa's pleas. Wet lips moved down to her neck while she writhed in his arms, struggling against his assault. I was certain he must have bitten her then, because Christa promptly cried out like a wounded puppy. That was all it took for The Boys to appear at her side.

The target barely had time to register The Boys before they were on him. Two sets of jaws clamped onto each ankle, puncturing the skin and biting into the bone. He squealed, pushing Christa away when the Fritz jumped up, sinking his teeth into the targets shoulder with a ruthless snarl.

The target tried to throw them off, barely landing a punch to one of The Boys heads. His attempts were feeble; chunks of flesh and fabric flew across the barn and, bit by bit, the target seemed to only grow smaller from where Petra and I sat. A few feet away, Christa seemingly cowered amidst the hay bales while blood began to seep out of his wounds and spatter across the barn.

A warbled scream rose from the thrashing body, only to be silenced when Ulf wrapped his jaw around the targets neck, puncturing his throat and silencing him once and for all.

Now standing over the lifeless body, The Boys looked up from their assault and turned their heads toward Christa, awaiting her final instruction.

"Good boys," she said and, standing tall, gestured a hand to The Boys to return to the vehicle. Once they had left the barn, Petra and I came out from our observation point and made our way to Christa's side.

"Are you ready for the next part of the plan?" I asked her. Nodding, Christa turned to Petra and smiled.

"Get on your knees, bitch," Petra instructed. She was far too excited for this; then again, she had just watched a man get ripped to shreds, and she had no part to play in it.

Falling to her knees hard enough to bruise them and cringing in anticipation, Christa readied herself for the first blow. Without hesitation, Petra curled her hand into a fist and smacked her on the side of her face. She did this a couple of times, making sure to bruise Christa's perfect skin and puncture her lips. For good measure, Petra grabbed Christa's hair and pulled out a couple of clumps to place in one of the targets dismembered hands.

Once Petra had finished, I proceeded to rip Christa's dress and tear off the buttons, adding to the illusion that she was almost raped. Who would question The Boys intent when they were only protecting their owner, who had been lured into the barn by a stranger? It was the perfect deception, and no one would suspect that it had been a double agent we had killed.

We drove back to the city with Christa at the wheel. We wanted to see if she could handle a beating and still function during a mission, so we had her drop us off before she went to find a local police station to make her statement.

Now safely back in our hotel room, Petra and I took out our list of targets and crossed the first name off.

With this part of the mission finished, we knew we needed to be gone. Swiftly, we packed our things and took the next train home, but not before making contact with Christa, where she ensured us that she would be driving home with The Boys.

We did not have time to get comfortable once we arrived home. After some hurried hello's to Auntie and the girls, we had a quick clean-up and a bite to eat before Petra and I had to make our way to Italy. Prior to leaving, Maria came to my room, lurking in the doorway while I packed.

"I would like to remind you that, *before* taking the targets out, you are supposed to be gathering intelligence on their handlers as well." Though she tried to phrase it as a reminder, the accusation in her words did not go unnoticed.

Without glancing up at her, I simply replied,

"Sometimes you have to react to a given situation." I closed my bag and stood to finally face Maria, glaring coldly at her. "It isn't always possible to follow instructions to the letter. *You* should know that." And without another word, I shoved past her through the door and made my way to Petra's room.

We arrived at the train station with ten minutes to spare. Once we had found our seats, we set to work on the finer details of our next target. This one would prove to be a little more difficult, only because the agent had deeply embedded himself within the Italian Resistance. Well respected and high in rank, it came as a surprise to us both that we had not come across him before during our past involvement with the Italian Resistance.

Nevertheless, this mission would have to be handled with care; we don't want to become enemies of the Resistance. These people could become important to us later on, depending on our development in later years. Creating a bond of trust in our business is difficult at the best of times, and we already have a good working relationship with the partisans in Italy, so we need to keep it that way.

Once we had fine-tuned the particulars of this target, Petra felt it was time for a nap. Far too awake from the day's activities, I took to the paper and caught up on current events throughout Europe.

The Allies are making solid progress Northwards, gaining ground every day in Italy. The partisans are constantly called upon to help the Allies in their endeavours.

Upon arrival in Italy and making contact with the partisans, we used our past experiences with them to enable us to join their group once again on their next objective. We stated that we were to report back to London on their progress, and to provide further support if required. To make this ruse seem more believable, we requested that the OSS provide an air drop of ammo and supplies to the partisans local drop-zone. This proved successful; the partisans are typically low in reserves, and so the extra ammo and supplies were gratefully received.

Whilst Petra settled in at the partisans camp, the local partisan leader pulled me aside. I immediately recognised him as our target and, without alerting him to my knowledge of who he was, allowed him to inform me of the following:

The Germans were all dug in at Bologna in Northern Italy, though a time frame could not be confirmed. The partisans would be the ones to infiltrate the city, causing as much mayhem as they could in an effort to soften the Germans positions prior to the Allied offensive on the city.

The partisans are already distributed around the city, and now it is simply a case of waiting for a short period of time before all Hell breaks loose. The scene has already been set, and it is the perfect opportunity for some friendly fire.

I went to collect Petra and, along with the partisans, we followed them to the city limits. Sticking close to the partisan leader, we followed his every move.

When the first bullet whistled through the air, more began to follow and quickly escalating into a full-blown skirmish. Soon the sky was filled with the chorus of agonising cries while the ground was littered with spent shells and the lifeless husks of fallen comrades.

In the fray of the fight, I nod to where Petra is standing and she makes her move; everyone is simply trying to stay alive, too preoccupied by self-preservation to notice our intentions. Dodging the bullets that fly past my head, I watch as Petra aims her sidearm and waits until the partisan leader finally turns back to face her, only to meet the barrel of her gun aimed at his head.

Petra doesn't hesitate and shoots before turning to attack the German lines, creating the illusion that the bullet in the partisan leaders head had come from the German side. With one less spy to worry about and our objective complete, we continued fighting off the Germans alongside the partisans, if only to ensure that our cover story stayed intact.

Once the last bullet had fallen to the ground, we re-grouped with the remaining partisans and informed them that we had to return to London promptly to give a report. We gave our condolences for their fallen comrades, including that of their leader, and after thanking us for our assistance, we took our leave while the partisans began collecting the bodies of those that had given their all that day.

We collect our stuff and make our way down from the partisans camp to the local train station. Once we are on the train home, Petra and I congratulate ourselves on another successful mission; that's two out of three targets killed, with both plans being executed to perfection.

Now we needed to prepare for the final objective; our last target will test our skills, that much I am sure of. Currently residing in Germany – Stuttgart, to be precise – the man is marked down as a triple agent in his file. He is also a high-ranking transport officer, overseeing all the transportation of troops and supplies within the South of Germany.

Germany is on high alert now as the Allies close in on all sides. Getting into besieged Germany will be easy enough; the hard part will not be getting killed by Allied bombers or artillery.

Once home, we gather our German papers and immediately head for the border. It is decided it would be more appropriate to go via Austria because, despite being the longer route, the access to the border was much easier and further away from the Allied offensives.

We arrived at Innsbruck, Austria. Already heavily bombed by the Allies, we moved swiftly to find a vehicle that we could commandeer. This seemed a little more difficult than we thought; most have been flattened by fallen rubble or have sustained direct hits, and those that are still running have already been taken by those fleeing the city.

We head for a place just outside the city where we know that the Austrian resistance is situated. Hopefully, they can help us.

Everywhere we go, every road is full of displaced families trying their hardest to carry whatever they have left and find a safe place to stay. They all look dishevelled, worn out, disheartened.

It took a few hours, but we finally found the resistance. They don't have much, but they share a little food with us and, while we ate and rested up, they head off to procure us some form of transport.

They returned with a couple of horses. Not sure about Petra, but I have not ridden for years. That's all they could find, however, and they also made it quite clear that any motor vehicle would be instantly commandeered by the Germans, so this was our best option. We gathered a couple of blankets and wrapped our gear in them, tied them to our trusted steeds to look as if we are part of the growing population travelling on these roads and were on our way.

It would take us a little over a day to get to Stuttgart on horseback. Throughout the whole journey, we saw and heard the Allied planes overhead. It seemed never ending. Relentless, even. There were a couple of times German troop columns would slow down when they saw or heard the planes coming. They knew they would be safe by using us as human shields. Once the planes moved on, so would they.

When we arrived on the outskirts of Stuttgart, most of the population had left the city for the relative safety of the surrounding countryside. We use this as cover to move around the outskirts to find the best vantage point.

After a quick survey of the city, we realised that it wasn't going to be easy getting in and out without coming head-to-head with German checkpoints and patrols. It seems like they are everywhere, and they are stopping everyone.

Thankfully, both Petra and I have original German papers, so we didn't have to worry too much about being checked. It was *why* we are there that is going to be the issue.

I went off to chat with some of the locals; we are going to need an honest reason for entering the city. I decided that I needed to find a fully displaced family, get their names and address and claim relation to them. Petra and I could then state that we are in search of my sister and her family, give them the address and, hopefully, that should get us through without issue.

We decided to get some rest when the sun was starting to set, aiming to head out at first light. I am not sure how these people can sleep through the constant noises of heavy artillery and planes in the distance. I guess they are simply use to it by now.

Before I knew it, the sky had grown light. I wasn't sure about waking Petra; we have no coffee, so she is undoubtedly going to be in a horrid mood. Still, I had very little choice in the matter, so woke her up and promptly walked away while she started to come around.

Upon my returned, Petra was ready but didn't speak. So, in silence, we began our short walk into the city and soon found ourselves at a checkpoint.

"What brings you here?" Asked one officer, while another grunted "Papers," beside him.

"I'm here to find my sister," I replied, handing them the necessary documents. "This was her last known location with her family. I must be sure that they aren't still at home."

The officers carefully looked over the documents, scrutinising every detail. Petra tapped her foot, more annoyed than anxious, when the two men finally handed the papers back to us, satisfied with their authenticity.

"You can go," said the one that had asked why we were there. "But we strongly advise against citizens entering the city; most of the citizens have already left, and I doubt your family will still be there."

I simply nodded my understanding and gave him the most pitiful smile I could muster. "I am aware. Still, it is best to be certain. I just want to know that she is safe."

Once we had entered the city, we could see that there were soldiers everywhere. Standing on every corner, peering out of abandoned houses and watching every step we made. This was beginning to look like a suicide mission for us; if we killed the final target and he was found, we would not get out of the city alive. This was going to require a much more silent approach.

We head for my sister's house only to find it, like the rest of the street, in ruins. For the sake of those soldiers watching us, Petra consoles me with a hug and then we search the rubble for anything personal to those that once occupied this home. Finding a family photo, in a smashed frame, I take it out and put it in my pocket. Slowly and with Petra linking arms with me, we negotiate the demolished street.

We headed for the targets place of residence first in the hope that he would still be there. Getting inside his home would be far easier than his place of work. Making sure to evade any wayward glances from the soldiers, we made our way towards the rear of the residence, hoping that that would provide us with a little more coverage, and found that one of the windows had been left slightly ajar. Giving her a boost, Petra managed to climb inside of the house and crept around until she could carefully open a door to let me in.

After surveying the place in its entirety, we find nothing; he hadn't returned last night. He was, however, still using this residence to rest in, that much was certain. All of his belongings were still in place and dust had yet to settle on his bed.

Petra and I make the decision to wait our target out for the day and decide to hide upstairs until he returned; he would need to change clothes, perhaps, or decide to gather his personal belongings before they were inevitably buried beneath the rubble of a ruined home. Besides, killing him during the night would provide us with a few more hours to escape before he could be discovered.

It turned out to be a very long wait; our target didn't return until 22.00. He ate something, bathed and went to bed. We gave it an hour to make sure he was sound asleep, only because he didn't seem to snore or breathe too deeply, so taking the time until we were sure he was asleep seemed to be our best option.

Once we were certain he would not wake up, Petra crept out of our hiding spot and took a quick look around, ensuring that we were alone. Once she had signalled that we were alone, I made my way towards our targets bed and retrieved my silenced pistol.

I shot him in the head. Twice, for good measure. Turning back to Petra, I nodded before heading towards the doorway. If we wanted to take the short route out of trouble, we would have to head East towards the forwarding Allied forces. That was our best bet.

Chapter Twelve

Hannah

We had made it through to the Allies, but it did take a few hours for them to verify who we are. Like the Germans, they don't really see females as any kind of threat. We did however provide the commanding officer with our codes so we would get a little help from them. They fed us and we re-stocked our ammo. It then took us several hours to get home, but we made it.

It was time to face the music with the OSS. They had stayed at their hotel until we confirmed completion of the task given. According to Maria, they are not very happy with us due to the fact we hadn't taken or even given any time to acquire the information they wanted.

They arrived at our home later that day.

"Well, that didn't quite go to plan now, did it?" Mr Smith says condescendingly.

"Look, this wasn't as straight forward as you'd think. We had to ensure that it couldn't be traced back to us in any way," I explained, placing both hands down on the kitchen table. "If the other government departments learn of our involvement, we could be in major trouble. Our first objective is our safety, *always*. That's the way it is."

"Very well. We can understand that." Mr Brown looked up at us through narrowed eyes while his hand curled into a fist. "It simply would have been nice to have their handlers, too. Nevertheless," he continued through clenched teeth, his head moving slightly to give a curt nod. "You have fulfilled your end of the deal. Here is the key, as promised."

He then slid the same clenched fist across the table and, opening his pink palm, dropped the slender piece of metal onto the surface. Standing from their seats, Mr Brown and Mr Smith collected themselves while Petra and I thanked them and, bidding our goodbyes, took the key and left them to have a chat with Maria.

Once we had exited the kitchen, I made my way to Mila and, handing her the key, asked her to collect the contents of the safe ASAP.

After Mila had left, I took myself away to find a quiet corner and catch up on the latest news and events. We are about to enter February, but it would seem that January has been a busy month already.

In the battle for the seas, there have been some loses on all sides. The RAF have dropped thousands upon thousands of tonnes of bombs onto the major cities of Germany. There has also been an earthquake in Mikawa, Japan, killing over two thousand people. The Allies in the Pacific are also making good head way against the Japanese. Then there was the liberation of the Auschwitz concentration camp.

The Soviets had found the camp which still had over seven thousand prisoners present. But that wasn't all; they had also found evidence of hundreds of thousands of Jews killed by the Germans. This isn't the only camp in existence, so I can't help but wonder what the final count of lost lives will be by the end of this horrific war.

Later that day, Mila came to find me.

"Hannah," she calls out, making her way towards me. "We have received an urgent coded message from London." She hands me the message, watching intently as I read through its contents.

"It would seem that the Americans are not the only ones with double agent issues," I explain. Looking up at Mila, I fold the letter and start making my way toward the kitchen with Mila in tow. "They want us to head back to Italy. It seems that the Northern Resistance has been compromised by two agents. Mila, can you go and find Petra for me, please."

Mila left me alone with a nod. Sitting at the table, I let my thoughts take over; had we caused this by killing the OSS agents? Did someone see us? Could they tell that it wasn't the Germans that had caused the partisan leaders demise?

It could also be nothing to do with us. It all just seems very timely.

Once Petra arrived, she sat down and we had a quick chat about my concerns. In the end, we decided to just go with it until we find out what is actually going on.

London had sent a plane to air drop us into Northern Italy; we just needed to get to our normal airstrip in France. The airstrip is only a couple of hours over the border, so, it didn't take long before we are in the air.

No matter how many times we do night drops, it doesn't get any easier. There are so many things that can go wrong. Night drops have a forty-five percent possibility of ending in death; being shot from the ground, hit by a flying bat, trees, buildings an even planes are just some of the most hazardous possibilities we could come across. It's truly difficult to keep these kinds of thoughts out of your head.

We safely hit the ground and check on each other as the resistance watch our perimeter. They then guide us by flashlight to our parachute hiding place that they had already prepared. We now have about an hour's hike up and around the mountain terrain to their HQ. The mountains still have some snow on them due to the height. In fact, even now with the right weather, snow can still fall.

To be honest, I am feeling a little apprehensive for the first time whilst meeting these people. They have had a hard struggle surviving in the mountains and they certainly don't like anyone who threatens them in any way.

Arriving at the hideout, we're greeted by their new leader. He meets us with a hot cup of watered-down black coffee. It had no flavour, but the main thing was that it was hot.

Hands firmly wrapping around our steaming cups, we follow him to his cabin; he has a blazing fire going and gestures for us to sit down. As he briefs us on the two double agents, Petra and I warm up by the fire.

"On several occasions, including some past missions, we have met with heavy German resistance," the leader explains, pacing back and forth while he speaks. "In some cases, my own men have been arrested prior to the start of a mission."

"And what of the two agent's involvement?" I ask, drumming my fingers against the warm cup.

"They were either on, or at least been made aware of all our missions upon their arrival," he replies with a frown. "They did, however, decline to live within the confines of our camp; instead, they both stayed in a small cabin further up the mountain. It's quite secluded up there due to the snow being constant all year round. In my mind, that makes them even more suspect. After all, who in their right minds would want to stay in such a cold, hazardous environment all year round?"

That does seem a little strange. Of course, it's still not concrete proof that these two men are double agents.

"Can you spare a guide to take us up there?" Petra asks.

The leader shakes his head. "Not at this time, no." He looks at us both, his lips pressing into a thin line. "We have our own mission and need every person we can get. I have, however, drawn you a map; it should only take you three or four hours to get up there." He produces the map and hands it to Petra, who promptly opens it to take a look. "I have also packed you some supplies and provided you bot with some ski's. You're going to need them."

He gestures towards a corner of the room where the provisions lay.

"Right. We will get some rest and set off at first light. Thank you for your help." I say before Petra and I went off to find somewhere warm to lay down for a while.

First light was upon us before we knew it. It was cold this morning but, then again, we are only in February.

After a little food and a hot drink, we set off up the mountain. It wasn't too long before we hit the first snow. We fitted our snowshoes that the leader had provided and continued onwards. The higher we went, the deeper the snow became. There was something quite satisfying about walking on fresh virgin snow; it's like walking were no one had ever been before and leaving our own mark.

The deepness of the snow did however make it difficult to follow the map; some of the landmarks were now hidden from view, meaning we could find ourselves easily lost.

Even with our snowshoes, the snow is now going up past our knee's; our trousers quickly become soaked through, only to freeze in the glacial temperature. This only proves to make our headway even more difficult. With each step we take, our legs seem to grow in size while the fluffy, bright new snow builds up around our icy trousers.

Every now and again, we have to stop and clear off our trousers before we can go again.

Neither of us brought a compass and, unluckily for us, we were not provided one by the leader, either. So, it's time to go old-school and make use of the sun. Once it popped out from behind the snow-heavy clouds, we began making our way out of the trees to get a much better idea of our surroundings. This took us longer than we thought it would; it's already been three hours and we should already have the double agents cabin in our sights by now.

We are lost.

Petra then remembers the radio that we have brought. We hope the agents have their radio on or, at the very least, that the resistance are listening. Switching it on, Petra presses the button to talk and asks if anyone is listening. She repeats this a few times, to no avail.

Gripping the radio tight in her hand, Petra turns to me with a snarl. "*Why* do you keep putting us in these situations? We are going to fucking die on this mountain, Hannah."

"It's not my fault, Petra," I reply tersely. "Now stop having a go at me and help get us out of this."

We eventually found a clearing and made a small camp to wait for the sun to pop out. We only needed a few seconds of it. The sun always rises in the east and sets in the west; a glimpse of it will provide us the correct heading. Using the snow, we built a wall around us to help shelter us from the cold biting wind.

Petra kept trying the radio but only in short bursts, as the Germans have now mastered the art of radio triangulation and the last thing, we need, is them after us. It's been five hours now and we are getting cold. It was too dangerous to make a fire but if something doesn't happen soon, we will have no choice.

Running out of hot drink, it was time to build a shelter and get a fire going. We broke out our knives and set to work and right on time, too, as the snow started falling again. This won't help anyone, as it would cover our tracks, meaning that we couldn't even follow them back down the mountain.

After building a small shelter using fern branches and overlaying them in a semi-circle, we place several of them on the ground to help keep our feet off the snowy ground. Building a fire isn't easy in this weather; thankfully, we had some dry sticks which the resistance had provided us. Using those to get the fire going, we collect thin branches from the trees around us; they take less time to cut and then dry out on the flames. Of course, we removed all the greenery to help keep the smoke down as much as possible.

Melting some snow for hot water, I filled the flask then warmed up a little food to keep us going. Another hour went by and still no sign of the sun, things are starting to look bleak. Petra and I chat a little about the prospect of spending the night on the mountain in a make shift shelter. It was decided that if we are to spend the night, then we will need more fire wood. We went of collecting the smaller branches off nearby trees.

I am picking up my bundle of wood when I hear Petra shout.

"Hannah, over here. Quick!"

Dropping the wood, I ran over to her as best I can in knee-deep snow. She was staring across the mountain. As I zeroed in on the area she was pointing to, it was our life line we are now both looking at; Smoke! Bellowing upward through the snow flakes. It could only be coming from the cabin we are looking for. We hurried back to camp and collected our things, put the fire out and headed off towards the smoke.

I focus on the area she was pointing and there, I see it: Smoke. Dark and thick as it curls through the falling snow. It has to be coming from the cabin we are looking for! *This* is the life line Petra and I have been searching for.

Hurrying back to the camp, we collect our things, put our own pitiful fire out and head off in the direction of the smoke.

The cabin is set in the centre of a small cluster of trees. The trees are not too dense and, if you stand a few feet away from the cabin, you can see in most directions and, most importantly, you can look down the mountain for quite a distance. This of course would be most people's approach. The back of the cabin nestled into the upward slope of the mountain, providing some strength to its vulnerable side.

Now, one thing we never want to do when approaching a cabin in the wilderness is head straight for the door. That's one way to get shot. Once we were about one hundred feet away, we stopped in our tracks and shouted towards the cabin.

"Hello! Is anyone in there?"

A man opens the door and stands in the opening, searching his surroundings for my voice. I shout again, louder, this time. "Over here!" and wave. Despite having no idea who we are, he still beckons us over.

As we get closer, I see his eyes light up; it's as if he hasn't seen a female in years. I wonder how he and his companion will react once Petra and I's coating of snow sheds in the warmth of the cabin? No doubt the same reaction as every male when faced with the opposite sex.

Taking a step closer, I shout out their code to identify ourselves as fellow agents.

"Brothers, ladies love red lipstick." The first part is their code name, the second part identifies us as female SOE.

"Come in out of the cold," he yells back, opening the door a little wider.

We enter and, sure enough, there is his fellow agent, sitting beside a roaring fire. He stands upon seeing us and, alongside his companion, aids Petra and I in removing our packs and ski's. We then start to peel off a couple more layers while one of the men makes us a hot drink.

"I'm Hannah and this is Petra"

"That's Karl and I'm Phillip," replies the man making the drinks, who then continues.

"What brings two pretty ladies this far up the mountain?" the one pouring water asks, glancing between us and the mugs. "We are not late with our transmissions, so it's not a rescue or reconnaissance mission, I assume?"

He hands one steaming mug to me and I take it, wrapping my freezing fingers around the hot vessel. "As we have now completed several missions here in Italy, London thought it would be a good idea to make personal contact with you both," I reply, subtly glancing over at the man by the fire who made little effort to hide the fact he was leering over Petra's curves and every move she made, however small.

"And what are *you* fucking staring at?" Petra snarls, glaring in Karls direction.

Both men's eyes grew wide, but Petra's words have the desired effect; Karl turned his gaze away from her to focus on something else in the room.

After a moment of silence between us, the agent making our drinks clears his throat, finally hands Petra a mug and asks,

"For what purpose?"

"Who knows," I shrug. "Maybe London has a joint mission in mind sometime in the future." My response is quick and hopefully enough for them both, though I am getting the impression both men are suspicious that something is not quite right.

"And what kind of mission could we possibly work on together?" asked Phillip as he hands his friend a mug before sitting on a stool near the fire. "You're females and certainly beautiful, yes, but I have no doubt you couldn't possibly work in a combative environment."

Petra and I exchange a look and a sly, undetectable smile with each other. The mindset of a man towards any female is fast becoming familiar with us.

They truly think they are the only sex capable of surviving during a war. It is this very mindset that can work to our advantage, though; if they think we are weak, it will only come as a bigger surprise when they inevitably find out what we are *really* capable of.

For now, we let their comment go, only because we don't want to spook them. Our goal here is to get rid of them as cleanly as possible, and without bloodshed.

It was getting late, so we made up a sleeping area on the floor near the fire. To their credit, the men – gentlemen of a kind, I suppose – did offer us their beds, but we decline. As we sort ourselves out, Petra and I make a quick survey of the cabin, looking for any and all weapons. We will also have to locate the men's radio; most agents don't have their radio where they sleep, but it's normally close by.

I notice they have the Sten and each a side arm, we didn't see any other weapons, but then we hadn't had chance to go through their packs.

After finishing our search, it's time to bed down for the night. One thing is certain; a night in the cabin with two drooling men that we can fight off, is still better than a night out in the open on top of a blustering, snow-capped mountain.

We woke early in the morning and I went outside for a quick smoke and some fresh air. Yes, it's a contradiction, but taking in the fresh, clean mountain air is always exhilarating first thing in the morning, even if I'm smoking whilst doing it.

Karl, the slightly younger agent of the two, was already up and chopping wood. When he saw me, we exchanged a short nod and a quick wave. As he carries the wood up to the porch, he informs me that they need to make their daily radio message to London.

"Would you like to come with us?" he asks.

"Of course," I reply with a smile.

We both head back into the cabin where we find Petra and the Phillip ignoring each other by the fire.

After more hot drinks and a little hot food, we prepare for the hike. If nothing else it, was nice to put on some warm, dry clothing again.

We all set off on ski's to their hidden radio. About ten minutes in, Phillip stops and states he needs to pee. While he shuffles off, Karl turns to speak to Petra and I.

"I think you should wait for him to return," he says and then proceeds to point into the distance. "The radio is just over the next ridge. I'll go ahead and wait for all of you to meet me there."

He sets off, leaving Petra and I alone on the mountain while we await Phillip to finish his call of nature. After a few minutes, it dawns on me that this is a rather long time for a man to take a piss; in our former line of work, I noticed various things about the male body, including how quickly a man can be when relieving themselves.

"Are you okay?" Petra called, but there was no answer. We look at each other. Something feels off; Petra and I are alone on a slope together, while Phillip is off somewhere. Where has he gone? We scan the direction he went in, looking for any signs of life.

"Do you think that this could be a trap?" I ask, squinting in the direction Phillip went. Petra shrugs.

"Perhaps," she replies, moving a few inches forward in the snow. Fuck, where *are* those guys? It's freezing! "Maybe they've figured out why we're actually here…"

Petra's words die against a loud *bang* that erupts somewhere ahead of us. The ground begins to shake beneath our ski's and like domino's, we go down.

I start clinging to the snow, wedging my fingers into its depths to try and find a rock or a ridge, anything to hold onto while the ground continues to shake. If those two men were meant to kill us, they were both poor excuses for assassins; they completely missed us with that blast.

Twisting on the ground, I turn to look at Petra who, like me, is clinging onto something beneath the snow. Except she's looking straight up at the mountain, her eyes wide and filled with unfathomable fear.

"…fucking *AVALANCHE!*" she screams, some of her words swallowed by the cascading snow that begins to tumble directly in front of us, and Petra struggles to get up from the ground.

I know Petra has spent many days on the slopes back home, so I am aware she has seen this kind of thing before. Once, she had told me of the danger it holds and the destructive power it can bring, and that it is not a memory so easily forgotten by those who have experienced it.

"Hannah, follow me!" she shouts again, spinning on her ski's once she is standing upright and heading in a direction, she considers safe. Scrambling to my feet, I follow Petra across the mountain and downwards, gaining some speed; she knows more about skiing and this situation than I do, and it seems like she has determined which way is the shortest route to safety. At least, I hope she has.

Bright, powdery snow was quickly gaining on us, reaching out and pulling us into its depths. The sheer speed of it almost bowled us over and, just as it hit, Petra took a sudden turn to follow its path, allowing the draught caused by the avalanche to momentarily give us speed. Then she took a sharp left, swerving across the mountain once again, but it's too late; the pure power and determination of the snow grips us both, pulling us from our ski's and dragging us beneath its frigid depths.

Everything turns white.

It takes a few seconds, but I hear Petra's voice. She's shouting something that I can't make out, but it's getting closer. Then I feel something grab me and *pull*, dragging me out of the snow until my eyes adjust and I can see the brilliant blue sky once again.

My breaths come out in uneven, shallow puffs as shivers take over my body. The world starts to spin around me, my heart hammering against my chest as I try to steady my legs, which are threatening to buckle from under me any moment now.

"Those fuckers tried to kill us, Hannah," Petra snarls, her head whipping this way and that. "Can you believe this shit? Once I get hold of them... hey, are you OK?"

The grip on my upper arm is firm as Petra steadies me, her focus now on my face and body. She frowns, giving me a once over.

"Nothing broken?" she asks. I don't respond; all I remember is snow, heavy and thick and *white*. So white, taking my breath away...

"Hannah..."

Her voice is muffled, just like when I was in the snow. The soft rumble of falling snow rushes through my ears, dragging me deeper...

"Hannah!"

Petra's shaking my arm, her face etched with worry. I shake my head and sigh, waiting for the noise to leave my head before I finally acknowledge her.

"I'm okay, Petra. I just need a minute," I assure her, though my voice sounds small. After taking in a few deep breaths of crisp mountain air, I look back at Petra who is watching me curiously.

"You saved us," I say. Indeed, the snow covering us hadn't been too deep; still, it was enough to scare someone who had never experienced it before now. "Can't believe we have just survived an avalanche!"

"Great, you're OK," Petra snaps, letting go of my arm. "But fuck having a minute. We're going after those fuckers." Throwing my snow-covered ski's at me with a glare, Petra begins putting her own on. "Put your ski's on, Hannah; at least one of those bastards is going to pay for this stunt!"

Once we our skis are secure, we head off in the agents last known direction. Petra is really pissed and is going far too fast for me to keep up, but I do my best. We occasionally stop to look for any fresh ski tracks and after fifteen minutes or so, we finally find some fresh tracks.

It has to be them.

I look back at Petra, but she's already following them. These are the only other tracks we have come across on the mountain, and Petra is one determined bitch. Without hesitation, I follow after her.

Petra

I don't give a shit if they are SOE; those fuckers tried to kill us. It's as simple as *'an eye for an eye'*, except they're actually going to die.

Those two have to be some of the worst killers I have come across. I mean, what the fuck? If you're going to kill someone, then make sure they're fucking dead before running off, at the very least. Total amateurs, the pair of them.

There is something to be admired about their plan, though; it's slight, but death by avalanche is quite a good move. It can easily be disguised as an accident, a natural disaster that claims innocent lives. Too bad they missed. They didn't even bother to stick around and make sure the job was done or think to finish the job properly.

Well, they will both see the errors of their ways once I catch up to them.

I am the first to arrive at a small village. Hannah is a little slow, but I am confident that she is OK. Kicking off my ski's, I start to search the perimeter and, after a few minutes, Hannah finally catches up to me.

"We should split up," I tell her, heading in one direction as Hannah dutifully walks in the other.

We scour all the public areas first, but there's no sign of them. Maybe those agents have friends here? If they've lived on the mountain for a certain length of time, it would make sense for them to know the locals. This won't be easy.

I have no time for pissing around. It's time to take a different approach.

I pull out my sidearm and kick the first door I come across. It flies open, swinging on its hinges as I hold my gun aloft and glare into the room. A man and woman sink back in their chairs at a wooden table, eyes wide and faces pale.

"Where are they?" I snarl, but all I get from the whimpering idiots are sniffs and stiff shakes of their heads. Clearly, they're not here; no normal citizen would be stupid enough to keep someone safe if it meant death for themselves. I back out of the house and stalk towards the next one.

I really should have deployed this tactic sooner; it's the most effective method for quick results. Cocking my gun, I ram my foot into another door and come face to face with an elderly woman.

"Two men," I hiss, aiming my gun at the centre of her forehead. "Where are they?"

The woman audibly swallows and with a slow, shaking hand, points towards her cellar. *Bingo.*

Nodding, I quietly step outside and draw out a sharp, loud whistle to get Hannah's attention. Given the fact the two agents have an advantage over me when alone, I think it's best to even the odds. Besides, those two bastards have Stens; all Hannah and I have are sidearms to protect ourselves.

Hannah soon enters the old woman's house and makes her way towards our hostage. Quietly, she instructs the woman to start boiling a large pan of water on the stove for some reason.

I motion to Hannah to join me outside for a moment. Leaving the door wide open, we keep our gaze and a gun trained on the elderly woman to ensure she won't do anything that might warn the double agents of our presence.

"The bastards are in the cellar. If we're quiet, we can sneak up on them both." I whisper. I can't have them hearing me, now. "By the way, why is she boiling water?" I point my gun at the woman who is watching us. Her eyes only seem to grow wider and she quickly turns around to watch the water boil.

"It's a distraction," Hannah explains with a shrug. "Once the water is hot, I will get her to pour it through the cracks in the floor and into the cellar. Once the agents start screaming, we'll open up the hatch and grab them."

I smile at the idea; a little torture before death is always good.

"Clever," I grin and move to go back into the house. Before I can enter the threshold however, Hannah grabs my arm to stop me.

"Petra," she starts, looking up at me with a frown. "We need at least one of them alive to take back to

London. He can be wounded, yes, but you can't kill them both. You can only kill *one* of them, not both. Okay?"

Shaking my arm out of her grasp, I roll my eyes and step into the house.

"For fuck's sake, Hannah, have a little faith," I bite back. "I'll kill *one* of them. Happy?"

She nods and quickly follows me inside to stand next to the old woman again, ascertaining how long the water will take. To be honest, I don't really care what London wants or if both men are killed. I have to pacify Hannah, though, otherwise she won't let me near them.

The water is ready after a few minutes, which means it's time to execute the plan and one of *them*. With a gun at her back, the elderly woman carries the pan towards the cellar door and begins to tip it forward. Water sizzles against the worn floorboards and cascades through the cracks, searing all that lies beneath.

Agonising screams quickly rise from below and the trapdoor is thrown open. Pointing our guns into the darkness, we send a hail of bullets into the void. Our shots are hopefully low enough so as not to kill anyone, if only to keep those bastards alive long enough for me to see the cowardice in their eyes before I shoot them.

When Hannah and I enter the cellar to grab the bastards, we come face to face with two pitiful, useless fucks cowering before us.

"Please," Karl the younger one sobs, shaking his head. "Please, don't... don't..."

I bark out a laugh; what happened to their confidence earlier, back when they sent an avalanche our way? After a little hot water, they have all but given up. How pathetic. It's no wonder these softies are double agents.

Cocking my gun at Phillip, I watch as he shrinks back, his eyes focused on the barrel. *Ha!* I could have these pathetic excuses for men dancing on one leg within seconds if I wanted to. I doubt there's very little they would do to have a chance at staying alive.

"Drop your weapons," I snarl, watching as they both do as their told. Putting my own sidearm away, I quickly grab both of the Stens and hand one to Hannah.

"Outside. *Now.*" I instruct. Grabbing one of the men while Hannah takes the other, we haul the pair out of the cellar and out of the house, ignoring the shaking woman as she watches us leave. Taking them away from the village and into the woods nearby, both men start babbling and plead for their lives.

"Please, you have to understand," Phillip hiccups, tripping over his own two feet as I drag him through the snow. "We thought you came to kill us. It was us or you. We're in a war; what else can we do?"

He's sobbing at this point, loud and annoying and pathetic.

I snigger at the sound and throw him against a tree. Hannah does the same for her agent while I hold my gun up to Phillip's head, the smile on my lips growing colder and wider as I watch him cower before my eyes.

"Well, you're shit," I tell him, eagerness clear in my voice. "You missed, and now you have *really* pissed me off."

Shaking his head, snot running down from his nose as his companion whimpers and pleads with Hannah, asking for us to just let them go. As if.

"Petra," Hannah whispers, standing close enough that I can hear, but far enough that her gun is still squarely aimed at the Karl's head. "Look at them; they're scared to death. We can't kill either of them, not now."

She shakes her head, pity in her eyes; bloody hell, she's going soft on me again! What's happening to the woman who tortured Otto?

Hannah steps a bit closer while I stroke my finger against the trigger. A hole would look so beautiful in that bastard's head...

"We have them both," she continues, one hand snaking onto my wrist. What is she doing? "Let's take them in. *Together.*"

Bang!

"Whoops," I say brightly, watching as Phillip's eyes roll into the back of his head while his body slumps the ground. "My finger slipped."

Letting out a sigh of displeasure, Hannah shoots me a glare while Karl's knees buckle beneath him. He drops to the ground, tears streaming down his face as he sobs loudly, shaking his head.

"Please. *Please,*" he chokes out, his body wracking with fear. "Don't... don't kill me, not me. It was all hi-his idea, a-anyway. Y-y-you got the right p-person..." I can barely make out the words through all his babbling, but I manage.

"You're not going to die," I tell him and grab his wrist to help him up. "Not today, at least."

I shoot him a grin and he only cries harder. I then twist him around, grab the back of his head and force him to look down.

There, with his mouth agape, eyes wide and bits of brain scattered around him lays his friends lifeless body, the once white blanket of snow now seeped in varying shades of red.

Leaning close to the Karl's ear, I clutch his hair harder and whisper,

"Behave yourself," I tell him, a soft chuckle escaping my lips. "Or you'll be joining him."

Chapter Thirteen
Hannah

It took a couple of days for us to get down the mountain. Once out of the snow-capped area, we strip our packs of anything we don't need, leaving them out in the open for anyone to find. Now a few pounds lighter, it doesn't take us long to arrive at our awaiting transport.

From there, it was only a few hours before the surviving agent was safely delivered to London in one piece. Well, his body was OK; I can't be sure about his mind, though.

We found somewhere to stay overnight, just outside the city; there was less chance of being bombed on the outskirts. We took it in turns to bathe, relishing in being clean again before getting ready for bed.

After a light breakfast the next morning, we head off to the airstrip to catch our flight back home. We have barely been back for a few minutes when Mila calls us for a meeting.

"I have recovered Otto's box," she tells us, excitement lacing her voice as she practically bounces out of the room to collect the contents.

Petra and I head into the kitchen and gather round the table with a coffee each, eager to see what contents had once lain within that box. A moment later, Mila walks back in with a brown leather case. Resting it on top of the table, she proceeds to empty it and lay everything out.

I catalogue the small handful of precious stones and a couple of gold bars. Finally, she pulls out a folded sheet of paper.

"Mila, what is that?" I ask.

"Something to brighten your day. In fact, it will probably make your week," she smiles, spreading the paper onto the table and carefully opening it in front of us. "*This* is the deed to Otto's Island, which means it is now officially ours."

Tapping the piece of paper, Mila looks between Petra and I, gauging our reactions. I can't help but smile; this *is* some of the best news I've had for a long time. Not quite as good as the recent announcement that the Allies are now taking back the towns and cities all over Europe, but it's close.

"This is great," I say, taking hold of my coffee cup and rising proudly from my chair. "Some of the best news I have heard today."

Petra and Mila follow suit, lifting their own cups in equal salute to our most recent accomplishment. Clinking the China together, we each take a triumphant sip.

Putting her cup down, Mila returns the contents into the satchel and pulls it closed.

"I will keep the stones and gold safe until Daphne can make a run," Mila says, turning around to leave as Petra and I finish our coffees.

For the rest of the week, Mila, Petra and I move around the grounds with joy evident on our faces. Things are good. Some of the newer girls are now fully trained up and ready to start contributing to our way of life, and though it's still undecided how we are going to move forward, we have certainly accumulated enough money and property to keep us all sustained for many years to come.

It has not escaped our notice that a very large proportion of the population has lost everything they have. Their homes, their families, even their dignity. Yes, we have tried to do as much as we can to help those in need, but is it really enough? Can we do more?

Money isn't everything, but if we can use what we have gained to help others, it can at least make a small difference for those who have lost more than they ever imagined.

I spent the rest of the afternoon sat in the garden with the boys reading a newspaper. It seems the war will come to an end soon; the Germans are retreating back into their homeland on all fronts, whilst the forces in Asia are beginning to take back solid ground from the Japanese.

We're coming up to March now and the first signs of the snow's thaw is upon us. The sun is gradually getting higher in the sky, it's light and warmth a little stronger with each passing day. I tip my head upwards and drink in the crisp late winter air.

The past few weeks have been quiet regarding missions from London. It has happened before, but now there are fewer coded messages coming through. There have even been days where we hear nothing from them.

We always thought this day would come. After all, Europe has suffered more than five years of tyranny from Hitler and Mussolini, the cost of which is ever present in the eyes of those who will continue to live through these horrors that, one day, they might eventually choose to share.

Europe will surely be at peace soon, and those left behind can start the tremendous task of rebuilding some kind of life.

I return to the house once I finish the paper. Mila is glued to the radio, constantly collecting information from any source she can find. She has also been stacking up quite the pile of intelligence; I think she's become a little obsessed in her quest to still honour Heidi's memory. Still, she is happy. I can't begrudge that.

As for the rest of us, we simply go about our daily routines. Petra and I have been visiting our many outlets around Switzerland, ensuring they are running well and placing some of the girls within any open positions. At this time, the main reason for this is to simply provide them with a sense of purpose, as well to take their minds off of their current situations.

On our visit, Petra and I finally agree on the direction we will be taking once the war is over, one that will include our newly multi-cultural team of well-trained ladies. However, if this plan is going to work, then we will need to have some of these girls undergo further education.

To this end, we have purchased a building in Zurich which is going to become a school for ladies. It is large enough to have several different classrooms as well as dormitories for them to sleep. It will be like a boarding school, but without the restrictions.

Looking at the positions held by women pre-war time, they were limited to working within the services, clerical work, teaching, factories, nursing and perhaps some shop work. Even after the war there is a high chance these will be the only positions open to women upon the men's return. So, we want to provide a chance for these women to have a choice of their preferred field.

We look forward to providing our girls with as much opportunity as possible after the war. A good education is important, and it will support them through these difficult times.

We have also started building two more Dorms on our land. Once these are complete, some of the girls who have already been trained in our basics will be tasked with filtering out across Europe in search of young ladies who have lost everything and bring them to us. No, these dorms will not be like orphanages; each and every one of them will become part of our family and receive the opportunity to train and school with us and, if required, housed and cared for by the rest of us.

It has also been decided that, upon their agreement, of course, a selection of our late teenage girls will travel and set up residence in countries like Australia, the US, Canada and so forth.

We will set them up with housing and a few months worth of funds while they start out doing any work available. The intention is for these girls to gain employment in their appointed country's top agencies, within the government and so on. It's a great opportunity that will allow them to move away from war-torn Europe while also providing them some much needed independence.

Now, having our own people living and working in different countries has its advantages. Though it won't happen at first, their real objectives will begin once they get their respective citizenships and have a solid foothold in a government agency job.

After some time, Mila eventually extricates herself from the radio to come and find me with some interesting news: Both the US and the Red army are actively searching for top German scientists as we speak.

On top of this, the US and Britain now have special units scouting for German plunder. Mila has also collected snippets of news that the Germans are hiding their ill-gotten gains in various tunnels, caves and old mines, and has even heard that they have dropped quantities of gold in large lakes.

"Anything of value has been moved or hidden," she explains, bouncing on the balls of her feet. "We are talking millions of pounds worth of art, gold and silver. However, I will note that the US are returning the art and sculptures to their countries of origin."

I nod; I can understand that. In fact, I agree with it. The gold and stones, however, are certainly fair game as far as I'm concerned. If Petra and I's plans are to last, then it will be good to get hold of anything we can find.

"Okay. Thanks for letting me know, Mila," I reply. "Do your best to keep track of anything you deem interesting, and be sure to update us as soon as possible."

We are halfway through March when we finally receive a mission from London.

"You are going to Berlin," Mila announces, gathering Petra, Auntie and I around the kitchen table. "London have sent word that your objective is to find the underground printing presses and put them out of action."

I frown; back in 1940, Joseph Goebbels founded the newspaper '*Das Reich*' merely as a propaganda tool. Despite this, he didn't actually have anything to do with the weekly running of the paper. He did, however, write a weekly column and articles for it. Almost all the articles in the paper were meant to deceive and boost the morale of the German people. In fact, Mila has several copies of '*Das Reich*', all of which we have taken to reading when we need a laugh from time to time.

It's important to tackle any and all aspects in war. If you can break the morale of a country's citizens, then that would be a major coup.

Mila and Auntie are not looking forward to me returning to Berlin due to the constant bombing of the city. I am confident the residents are surely broken by now. Still, a job is a job and I guess it's better than sitting around here on the sidelines, merely listening to the radio and reading the papers for updates.

Petra, however, is rather jubilant over the news. Grinning, she says, "If you can't kill them with guns or poison, then *blow the fuckers up!*"

Our plan is to make our way to Berlin, however we won't be travelling by train; it is not a very safe method nowadays. So, we are going to make our way by vehicle.

We anticipate that we are going to encounter some high defence check points along the way. With Petra coming from Berlin herself, we can use that a ruse to make our way into the city. This method worked for us beforehand, so it's our hope that it will work again.

One of our girls takes us to the border using one of our own cars. We then cross into Germany and meet up with the resistance who have procured us alternative transport. It's going to take us several days to arrive in Berlin, and it is certain that this journey is going to be one of our most hazardous.

Mila has provided us with a map of the paper's substations along our route. It seems that Goebbels has it all planned out; he wants everyone to be reading the paper on the day of publication. To this end, printing presses have been established in most major cities throughout Germany, enabling a swift delivery of new prints to a person's homes.

Now, it's not going to be possible to take them all out, but we know that all of the printing presses are all linked to the main office. So, we will cut off the proverbial snake's head and let the body die. Besides; the Allies are constantly bombing almost every major city these days, so it is possible that these printing presses are no longer standing unless, similar to the one in Berlin, they have moved underground.

The redeployment of supplies and manufacture into underground complexes, tunnels and the like has been an ongoing objective of the Third Reich for a couple of years now. This decision was made by Hitler as a direct result of many losses of key manufacturing plants over the past years.

We are under no illusion about this mission; the British send over reconnaissance planes constantly, but you can't beat good old eyes on the ground.

After a few hours of travel, we arrive at Stuttgart. As expected, entering the city was no issue; the Germans are far more interested in building defensive positions in readiness for the Allies.

Driving through the city, we can see no signs of anyone standing on street corners with the '*Das Reich*' paper. In fact, there are no street corners left for people to stand on; most of the city is now raised to the ground, meaning that navigating the streets was quite difficult. I can only guess that most of Stuttgart's residents have since fled to the countryside for safety.

The city has changed so much since our last visit a couple of months ago. With the Allies continuous bombing, this once beautiful city has been left it in ruin.

It seems like I will never get used to the smell and sound of a city that is constantly being bombed. We see a few people aimlessly wandering the ruined streets, their broken screams a plea for help.

Dead bodies left to rot now litter the road. The air is cloying, an acrid smell of smoke and dust particles searing at my nostrils. Beneath that lies the lingering scent of burnt flesh, hanging around the remnants of Stuttgart like death's cloak.

The horrors of war has left this parting gift to us, the sights and sounds a horrible memory that will stay with all its survivors until the day we die.

We keep on driving and eventually make our way out of the city. I find somewhere to park for a few minutes and jump out of the car with Petra following suit. Lighting a cigarette, I lean against the car door, the gaunt faces of those still roaming the streets in my mind while the lingering scent of death continues to wrap itself around me.

I am German, yet witnessing the downfall and destruction of our once great country and its cities is… it's hard. Of course, I feel deeply about it. Indeed, I make it no secret that I have no love or any kind of affection for the Third Reich, but my country is still my country. Much like most of the population, I am – No, I *was* – proud to be born here. Now, I am unsure.

Finishing my cigarette, I go for a quick pee before we set off towards Nuremburg in silence.

Most of this journey has been spent in quiet, actually, but what else can be said that we haven't already discussed? Constantly returning to those same thoughts and feelings isn't going to change anything, after all, and only serves to re-enforce the memories that we want to forget.

Nuremberg is our overnight stay. Mila has already made the arrangements for us to link up with the local resistance. If we could find a hotel to stay in – if any of them were still standing, that is – then we would, but there is no chance in Hell I am going to put myself through another potential bombing; I can't risk being trapped or buried alive again.

I will not be able to sleep in a hotel. No, it will be safer and certainly more productive to stay with the resistance and gather what any intelligence they can provide.

Once we arrive at our location, the resistance promptly informs us that they haven't seen the *'Das Reich'* paper in Nuremberg for at least two weeks. I'm not surprised; the city is in total ruins, much like Stuttgart. There is hardly a building left standing that doesn't have any lasting structural damage caused by the bomb blasts or fire.

There is little to report, so once Petra and I have been updated on the current news, we get our heads down for the night.

The next morning, Petra and I sip coffee we have brought with us while we discuss the possibility of this being a futile journey.

"It isn't inconceivable that London are attempting to put us in harm's way," I mumble, nursing my cannister. "We know too much."

Of course, this could simply be my imagination running wild; the mere thought of travelling through Germany whilst the Allies are on a rampage sets my nerves on edge, and there is no denying that will fuel my anxiety.

We finish off our coffee and leave. We are heading for Leipzig today and, despite it not even being 09.00, I can already hear the Allied planes overhead. It's like a running gauntlet every hour as one of us drives and the other watches out for the planes.

The closer we get to Berlin, the worse it is. The noise around us is constant, starting with the shuddering engine of a plane just minutes before the loud *thud* and *thump* of their payloads can be heard, dropping to the ground and successfully finding their targets.

If it isn't bombs dropping from the air, then it's the large shells from cannon fire ringing in the distance while both sides fight for every inch of ground they can claim. It's constant, an everyday event occurrence of churning engines mixed with the trill of artillery and deafening explosions to create this catastrophic cacophony.

Death is something that happens to us all; it's just a case of when and where. I have no issue with death, and I am sure the same can be said for Petra. If we die doing something we believe in, then so be it. It's more about how I go that bothers me.

If I go fighting for my life, then gladly. It's simply survival of the fittest, after all. But if I'm taken out because of a stray bomb there is no honour in it for me.

The roads are quickly becoming impossible to navigate. If we aren't stopping for fleeing residents, then it's for the retreating army who bully and push their way through the masses. Like Moses parting the Red Sea, people of all ages are using every ounce of strength they have left to move out of the way of on-coming vehicles. As they retreat, fear and desperation seems to fuel them while the Germans refuse to slow down for the children or even the elderly.

As we slowly approach Leipzig, we are stopped by a soldier.

"Leipzig is closed," he yells, his voice booming over the noise of the crowd. "The city is unsafe to enter."

We begin our own retreat as Petra smacks her hand against the car door.

"Shit!" she hisses, now slapping the dashboard. "This is fast becoming a fucking waste of our time and effort, Hannah."

I can feel her glare on me from her seat while I keep my eyes on the road.

"We need to find a way around the city," I say simply.

"Fuck's sake, Hannah," she snaps and from my periphery, I see her stab a finger at the window. "There is nothing left of these cities. Why are we chancing our lives for these fuckers? I reckon they are trying to get us killed! Fuck um all, let's go home."

"Petra, stop with moaning," I bark, wrenching my eyes from the road to glare at her. "Just help me get us to Berlin. *Now.*"

Despite her grumbles, Petra begins studying the map and after a few minutes, tells me to turn around and take the first left turning about four miles down the road. It adds about an hour to our journey, but Petra directs me to alternative roads around the city. Thankfully, she seems to know the area very well.

The smaller villages we pass through have not been able to hide from the Allied bombings. Each one is just as devastating as the last. Beautiful, small buildings, homes that have housed generations are now nothing more than rubble and smoking timber.

We pass through another village turned to ash when Petra screams *"STOP!"* and I force us to a screeching halt.

"What the hell, Petra?" I scream back, except she's not paying attention to me and instead looking out the window.

"Look," she says, pointing towards one of many piles of rubble. "Over there. *Look.*"

She sounds desperate, her voice falling unusually quiet. I know Petra wouldn't ask me to stop unless she truly meant for me to, so I gaze out the window at where she's pointing if only to humour her.

At first, I see women, all of them moving in rows while they search through broken homes and smashed brick. They're searching for their loved ones, I suppose, a harrowing task that only results in heartbreak.

Then I see it, the reason Petra stopped me. There, close to the debris of a fallen home kneels a young girl, her body wracked with sobs and her cheeks stained with tears. Even from afar, the echo of her cries pierces the air while she clutches at the bodies lain out before her, all neatly placed in a row.

Her family, surrounded by the ruins of what may be their familial home and their final resting place.

Without warning, Petra jumps out of the car and makes her way towards the girl. I follow in haste but, to my surprise, Petra doesn't stop. Instead, she walks right past the girl and barely spares her a glance as she walks up to the women closest to us.

While she talks to them, I stop in front of the girl who, upon sensing my presence, sways forward into my open arms.

"T-they were all I h-had," she hiccups, burying her wet face into my chest while I hold her close. "W-what am I going t-to d-do?"

Coughs and sobs take over her small, trembling body while I gently rock her back and forth, hoping to soothe her. The girl is filthy, cloaked head to toe in dust while cuts litter her skin and bruises start to bloom on her arms, legs and chest. Her clothing is marred with holes and black char marks while her hair clumps together with dry blood.

My body stiffens against hers, that familiar scent of fire and smoke scraping against my nostrils. A lump forms in my throat as I remember the cellar, dark and unyielding. Our experiences might not be similar, but this girl has also endured hardship and torture, wondering if she would die to the twisted hands of fate or maybe live to tell the tale of a country brought to ruin.

After a few moments Petra finally comes over to crouch beside me and the girl. Gently, she reaches out a hand and begins to stroke through the matted strands.

"This was her only family," she says quietly, her eyes trained on the girl whose shaking begins to calm while she lays in my arms. "They were on the road passing through. No one knows who they are."

"Petra, we can't take her," I say just as softly. "We're going through some dangerous places. Taking the girl with us could be... well, it's suicide, really."

"Don't lose your sense of justice now, Hannah," Petra scolds me, her gaze tender as she stares at the girl whose sobs have somewhat quietened. "She can't roam the streets, not like this. Those women can't care for her, they said so themselves."

 and she certainly won't be able to dodge those bombs alone."

"It's dangerous..." I start, but Petra cuts me off.

"She will be safer with us," she says, her gaze meeting mine. There is determination in her eyes. "She won't be able to dodge those bombs alone, not like this. Besides, when are our missions ever safe, Hannah?"

I let out a heavy sigh; Petra has a point.

"When did you grow a heart?" I ask begrudgingly, though I can't be mad; Petra is doing the right thing. "Fine. *Fine*, she can come with us. Help me get her to the car."

With Petra's help, we guide the girl to the car and sit her on the backseat. We clean her up as best we can and give her a little food and water and soon enough, she is lying back in the car as we drive off while she falls asleep.

It isn't long before we are on the outskirts of Berlin. From what we can see, there is hardly a building left standing. It also seems impossible that we can drive any further, so we head towards what was once a small farm about a quarter of a mile away. There we can safely leave the girl in hiding whilst Petra and I enter the city on foot.

As we approach the farmhouse, I can already see that it's home to what seems like a rather large population of people. I'm not surprised; a standing building is precious during these times of war where nothing is permanent. What does surprise me, though, is the presence of guards.

At least I think they're guards, but only because they seem to be on sentry duty. What are they doing here and why aren't they fighting? Why aren't they in full uniform?

"Stay with the girl," I say while turning to Petra as my hand reaches for door handle. "I'll find out what's going on. Okay?"

Thankfully, Petra readily agrees and arms herself with a few weapons, just in case. Swinging the car door open, I step out of the car and make my way towards the farmhouse.

I slow myself to a gentle stroll. I can already see that my approach hasn't gone unnoticed; two guards are carefully watching me while the others look to be readying their weapons for attack. Really? Do they see a single female as a threat?

As I move forward, I can clearly see that many of these men are injured in one form or another. Some of them are lying down, their wounds gaping while they groan and cry for help.

I keep moving forward until one of the guards barks out,

"Halt!"

I stop in my tracks at his demand.

"What do you want?" he snarls. Standing tall, I look him in the eyes and clear my throat.

"My friends and I are looking for a safe place to bed down for the night," I begin, my voice soft and small. Hopefully, my womanly ways will make the man more amenable to my plight. "You have nothing to fear; we are just two females and a young girl."

Before the man can reply a loud, booming voice comes from somewhere inside the house.

"Let her through," someone says and, cocking his rifle, the guard beckons me onward.

Twisting my head around, I can see an open window close by. Perhaps someone saw me from there? Turning back, the guard and I carefully approach the doorway, ensuring I don't stand on anyone. Entering the house, I see every inch of the floor, the furniture and even the staircase is covered by injured bodies. Some of them even have a buddy tending to their wounds. Picking my way through the pile of semi-conscious, maybe even unconscious bodies, I struggle through the house as I hold my breath, trying my best not to drink in the lingering scent of death.

Further ahead in the room I catch sight of a man. He's wearing what seems to be a once white doctor's coat, except now it is frayed and splattered in crusty spots of maroon. As if he could sense me coming, he looks up from the body he is currently tending to.

"Over here, girl. Quickly," he shouts and, as quickly as I can, I make my way over to him. "Push this wound until its closed, now. I need to sew it up."

I do as he instructs. Crouching next to the body of yet another man, I push the wound together until it closes while he sets to work.

"My friends and I are looking for a place to spend the night," I explain, watching the needle puncture the whimpering man's flesh, the thread tightening as his wound slowly comes together stitch by stitch. "We won't bother anyone. We just need somewhere until the sun rises tomorrow."

Grunting his understanding, the doctor nods. "If you can find a spot, you're welcome to it."

I pause for a moment and survey the area quickly. Death surrounds this home, even if it has yet to claim some of these men. I don't think I can leave the young girl here, not when she's seen her own family die right before her eyes. It's simply unfair, perhaps even cruel.

Once the doctor finishes sewing up the man, I rise to my feet and wash my hands before quickly heading back to the car.

"The place is full of injured and dead soldiers, Petra," I explain the moment I reach the car. "This is no place for a girl who has just lost her family."

"Then what the hell do you suggest we do, Hannah?" she asks, raising an eyebrow while I slide into the driver's seat and grip the wheel. I take a moment before I realise where we are. Perhaps there *is* somewhere safe to leave this girl.

"Perhaps we should drive to my old neighbour's home? If she's there, we can probably drop the girl off while we finish our mission."

"Worth a shot," Petra says with a shrug as I start the car.

Within thirty minutes or so of driving we approach my old neighbour's home. Pulling up, I can see that the place is now overgrown and could do with a little attention and care. Well, I suppose she is far too old now and, since the death of her husband, she has perhaps lost motivation to do anything.

Much like she was a few years ago, I can see her sitting on the front porch in the same chair. She's even wearing the same clothes, I think. Now, though, she's just as frail and rickety as her chair.

I jump out of the car while Petra opens her door and heads round the back of the car to get the girl. Walking towards the house, I wave over at the woman.

"Hello," I call out, loud enough for the woman to hear. "It's Hannah, your old neighbour! I was a friend of your daughter."

The woman looks up at me for a long moment, her gaze unblinking while she takes me in. Then, finally, she offers a small wave in response and inclines her head forward.

With her quiet invitation, I walk up to the porch and smile down at her. Indeed, these are the same clothes from when I saw her last, though they are fraying and duller in colour.

"Shall I make us some tea?" I ask. The woman smiles at the suggestion.

"Please," she says, gesturing towards the door. I make my way into the house and prepare the water for boil while I look for the cups. As I set about my task, the old woman walks into the kitchen with Petra and the girl close behind.

"It has been a while," I hear the woman say while chairs scrape back against the floor and everyone seats themselves. "So, I can only wonder what brings you here, young Hannah, and with friends, too."

I start pouring the water into four cups and nod. Of course she might be curious; we have not seen each other for years, now. Handing a cup to the old woman before I serve Petra and the girl, I finally grab my own and settle onto a chair at the table and turn to my former neighbour.

"We need a place to stay," I begin. "Specifically, we need a place for this young lass to stay. Petra and I have business to deal with further afield, is not safe for one so young. Not on these roads."

I look over at the girl. She is quiet, a contemplative look on her face while she stares down into the steaming tea. She does not look up when I mention her, nor does she make a sound to acknowledge her agreement.

Thankfully, the old woman is rather keen on this idea.

"Of course she can stay with me, Hannah," my old neighbour smiles, setting her cup down on the table. "I will be glad for the company."

I breathe a sigh of relief. As we finish off our tea, Petra and I make small conversation with my neighbour before bidding our goodbyes and leaving the girl there, safe and with good company.

We head straight to Berlin from there and, once we approach the border, we shut off the car and hide it behind some nearby bushes just on the outskirts before making our way into the city.

We walk through the remnants of fallen architecture, the history of a once beautiful place now lost to Hitler's legacy of ruin.   Berlin has gone. What once stood as the pride of our country is now nothing but ashes and debris, a graveyard of all it had once been.

It is going to take years to rebuild, but it will never be the same. The history we held will never be seen or admired ever again.

In the coming years people will not be saying that Germany has once again become a great nation. No, instead they will be discussing the total devastation and persecution of the Jewish population and other selected people. They will remember the thousands upon thousands of people that gave their lives while they relay each and every brick whilst cities are rebuilt, the needless deaths of families whose generations have all but been wiped out. All of this for what? Something that the Germans never asked for, a *'Living Space'* that was already inhabitable before Hitler ruined everything.

In my opinion, this was all simply a smoke screen to hide a narcissistic, power hungry, race-hating little man.

We enter what is left of the street where the newspapers head office once stood. Of the people we do see, we can't see anyone reading a paper while we make our way through the city debris. We stop a local to ask about it.

"The last edition came out last week," he tells us. "The next paper is due out today, but the printers seem to only leave a few bundles of the paper out wherever they can."

It seems people are too scared to stand on the streets selling them now. Thanking the man, Petra and I move further into the city. All we have to do is look out for someone carrying bundles of papers and follow him back to the printers. As walking is our only viable method of transport while navigating these streets, I don't think keeping up with them will be much of an issue.

We spent the next couple of hours scanning the skies for planes and listening out for the familiar sound of dropping bombs. Our hope is that, when one comes, we will run in a different direction to their flight path. Hopefully we won't get caught out by one before we find a paperboy, though.

Thankfully no bombs have fallen yet and, walking through a particularly dusty area, Petra and I finally spot him. A young lad of about twelve or so, a bundle of papers in his arms. He looks this way and that before finally dropping them on the ground and turning to leave.

Following him, the young lad leads Petra and I to an underground labyrinth of tunnels. Why aren't these being used as bomb shelters? They look deserted outside of the clattering machinery that purrs with life, the only real indication that anyone has been down here recently.

Unbeknownst to him, the lad takes us further into the depths of the labyrinth until we reach a small room. Housed within it are a couple of women turning out the paper, their faces gaunt and eyes blank, not a sound daring to pass their lips.

"It's time to leave," I shout. One by one, everyone looks up, their eyes growing round with fear. "Take all the young ones with you and don't come back." Taking out my gun, I point it towards one of the women while Petra aims hers at the young lad.

They do not move. Finally, Petra cocks her gun up and *bang!* A warning bullet rings through the air.

"Get the fuck out of here!" she snaps, pointing her gun back at the lad. *"Now!"*

That does it. Scrambling to leave, the women grab the young ones in a hurry and leave the room. Once we are sure everyone has safely exited the tunnels, Petra and I began planting the explosives we had brought with us before setting each one of them off and hurrying back to the surface.

We stood a good distance away while we wait. It only takes a few minutes, but the moment they go off is obvious. The street that lies directly above the room begins to shake, pebbles and broken stone bouncing and skittering across the ground while some of the damaged buildings begin to crumble further and deposit more of their already falling structure onto the street below.

Thankfully there are hardly any soldiers around. Thankfully, of the few we have seen, none of them care enough to take notice of us.

Dust covers us from head to toe as we make our way out of the city. Collecting our car, we set off once again to my old neighbour's house to collect the girl.

We have only been gone for a few hours and upon arriving at the house, I see the young girl on the porch. She's playing quietly with a doll while the old woman sits in her chair, staring out into the fields.

I stop in my tracks. I recognise that doll. It was my friends once, before she became lost to the hands of this cruel world.

"Hannah?" Petra asks. I shake my head and keep going, making my way to the old woman while Petra goes to the girl.

"Thank you for taking care of her," I tell my old neighbour and lean down to pull her into a hug. She holds me tight for a moment, her hair coming up to pat my head as she sighs.

"Take care, young Hannah," she whispers. Nodding against her shoulder, I finally pull back and step away.

Turning around, I nod to Petra. The young girl is holding her hand while the doll lays in the crook of her arm. With wide eyes, the girl looks back at the old woman who kindly smiles.

"You can keep it," she says. "The doll has been lonely without a friend for a long time, now."

I blink, my eyes stinging for a brief second. Shaking my head, I lift my hand to the woman and smile to her, perhaps for the last time.

"Farewell," I say softly.

Returning to the car, Petra helps the young girl climb into the back while I look towards the house. It might seem cruel to leave the woman here, but when I first came back to visit years ago, we had already discussed the idea of me taking her away. She doesn't want that, though.

"This is where I want to die," she had told me, a sad smile ghosting the corners of her mouth. "It is where my husband and your parents are, young Hannah. I wish to be buried alongside them, to always be by their side even in death."

I can only respect this wish of hers. With one final glance towards the house and the silhouette of a kind old woman sitting in her chair, I get back in the car and begin to drive away.

We need to get home and out of Germany as fast as we can. We decide to head for our training facility to see if there is a plane still on the airfield.

"If there isn't a pilot, I can fly us down to Austria," Petra says. Twisting my neck, I turn to stare at her.

"I didn't know you could fly?" I say. Turning my attention to the road again, Petra lets out a dry chuckle.

"I can't," she says brightly. Oh, shit. "I've seen it done before, though. How hard can it be?"

My blood runs cold. I don't know which one is scarier; travelling back by car through an ongoing battlefield, or having Petra attempt a new skill. The possible outcome is the same for both, though; it's just a case of which one will bring me swiftly into the afterlife.

Chapter Fourteen

I was thankful there was no plane when we arrived at the airfield. Continuing our drive, it took us three days to get home; we took the long way round, instead going through Poland and down to Austria as we made our way towards Switzerland.

Once home, we inform Mila of our success and help the young girl to settle in with Auntie. While Petra and I go to clean ourselves, Mila leaves to inform London with a simple message:

'Success.'

Over the next few weeks, we all keep a close eye on the papers. Each and every one of us at home are reading with eager anticipation. Mila is constantly stuck in the radio room, listening to every broadcast that comes on, but not just from Switzerland; she now has several radios on hand, each one tuning into a different countries broadcast.

Well, 'radio's' is not exactly correct, as Mila likes to tell me. They are in fact 'radio receivers', and are only one part of the latest equipment within the room. Mila has been able to gather herself an impressive collection recently, one that can rival any military communications station. Even the radio tower that now stands proudly atop one of the out buildings is a sight to behold, standing as tall as the Eiffel Tower.

Now she can listen in on everyone's open radio chatter. Enlisting the help of some of the other girls, Mila assigns each of them different frequencies to listen to.

Heidi would be so proud of her.

April 10th 1945

This is turning out to be the beginning of the end for Hermann Göring. Mila has picked up on some chatter; he is packing up all his belongings and treasures at Carinhall, his hunting lodge estate North-East of Berlin and transporting them down to Berchtesgaden, Bavia in South-East Germany on the border to Austria, just nineteen miles from Salzburg.

The reason for this sudden move is that the Red Army are quickly closing in on his residence. If they catch him, he will of course make a great trophy for Moscow's display, but like the drugged-up coward he is, Göring is packing up and moving to his southern residence.

Luckily for us, that means he is right within our reach; it's an opportunity we can't miss. The man has bought, stolen and even killed to accumulate some of the greatest art and jewellery from around Europe, so perhaps it's time for some payback before the Allies have a chance to reach him.

Once Mila finishes updating me, I gather some of the girls together and we set to work. We discuss all the possibilities open to us, how we can get it and out as quickly as possible while stealing as much as we can.

"And we can kill a few fucking Germans, too," Petra adds eagerly.

"That is secondary to the main objective, Petra," I remind her sternly. "Hitting Göring where it hurts by taking his beloved collecting will devastate him and do more harm than a blow to the head."

Over the next few days Mila collects as much information as she can regarding the surrounding area and his residence. A plan is forming and soon enough we have something solid in place.

Göring will most likely have minimal staffing and guards on-site, we think, as most soldiers are currently fighting for their country on the front lines. Even if that isn't the case, the risk is worth it in our mind.

We will arrive at the residence and do a full reconnaissance of the building from all angles. This will ascertain the number and strength of the guards. Can they be taken out swiftly and quietly?

If Göring is there, then we will probably just kill the fucker, as Petra puts it. Though it's not the main part of our plan, I do agree with her sentiment. He will only get in the way if we keep him alive.

We can probably accomplish all of this within a couple of days. On the surface it seems relatively easy; get in and steal things, get out and go home. Done. But as we have learnt during previous missions, nothing is ever as easy as it looks, and it certainly doesn't always go to plan.

Next, Mila, Petra and I select a couple of girls who will join us before making our way to the Austrian border. Once we arrive, we head straight for the town of Berchtesgaden. After locating his residence, we set out to complete a full reconnaissance of the surrounding area to ensure we have a solid escape plan in place.

We split up next, completing a re-con of his residence as we head to our individual sides to form a square-like pattern around Göring's home. We make a map of all the guards and staff's movements, gaining an understanding of the layout and where the guards especially patrol.

We are already aware that the main staff will offer the least resistance; even for the people they serve, they won't want or even have a desire to fight. Still, it's good to evaluate everyone within the target area, regardless of their loyalty to our target.

We use the next six hours to observe. Then, just after sunset we rendezvous at our pre-arranged location to evaluate our findings.

We have eight guard's; each one allocated a patrol area. Some of them can be taken out silently and away from the other guards line of sight. Looking at our map, we decide that we will be able to remove the remaining guards in pairs.

It's dark now. Once we are all set, we take up our respective positions. As each of our designated targets enter their respective area, one by one we strike with a swift, single jab of a knife to the neck, followed by a full, sharp cut across the throat. They drop like flies with a quiet gurgle of their final breath.

We have to move quickly; the other guards will soon realise that their compatriots are missing. Now coming together in pairs, I join one of the girls as we swiftly move to take out the remaining guards. In under five minutes, all eight of them have fallen; not too bad, considering two of the girls we brought with us are new.

Entering the house, we make our way through the rooms and begin to round up the staff. So far, none of us have seen Göring. One of the girls takes the staff into an empty room while the rest of us begin to search the entirety of house, ensuring we haven't missed any staff members. Thankfully, it seems we have gathered everyone already.

Upon returning to the room, our girl informs us that Göring is not at home. Apparently, he isn't going to arrive until tomorrow.

We can't wait for him; we have to move and be long gone before daybreak. We tie up and gag the staff, lock the door to the room they are in and systematically search the residence, each taking a room and clearing it of anything of value.

It takes about an hour to completely search the residence. Once we meet in the lobby again, we start dividing the spoils and packing them away. Money, jewellery and gold go into three separate rucksacks. The paintings are much bigger, so we roll them up and decide to transport them together so that they won't be damaged during the trip back home.

Once everything has been sorted, we ready ourselves to go home, but not before leaving Göring a few parting gifts behind.

Having someone on our side who not only works in intelligence, but also collects and keeps everything is pretty handy. Mila owns an impressive supply of military booklets, leaflets and so on. One of these pamphlets – No. 21-23 and produced by the US – is titled *Mines and Booby Traps*, and was originally produced in November 1944. It's one that I am pleased to have spent time perusing over in my spare time, as it has enabled me to learn a few new tricks for our good friend Göring.

Taking out the grenade trip wires we brought with us, we set them up around several doors. We then begin placing a few German TMiZ teller mines around the house, hoping that at least one of these traps might catch Göring out upon his return.

Satisfied with our trap placement, we finally leave and in less than a day we are home. Everyone is happy with the outcome of our mission and once inside, we begin to inspect the contents of our haul.

Daphne has since selected and trained several of our girls, all of whom are now capable in finding the value of each and every item that comes through our home. It seems as if we now have a stolen merchandise division, too, with each of the girls consolidating their knowledge in their desired subject; art, stones, silver, gold and so on. Dividing the spoils into each category, the girls begin to then inspect and evaluate it before passing their findings onto Daphne, who decides which one of her contacts is best suited to sell it to.

I am honestly impressed with their work. They are all highly efficient, and Daphne has done a wonderful job training them.

We are almost one hundred strong now, with girls from many different countries having joined us. Admittedly, all of them at different stages of training but every week, more and more are proving themselves in the field or at home. Things are shaping up very nicely.

April 27th 1945

Mila comes rushing into the kitchen full of excitement, insisting we follow her to the radio room. As we make our way to the room, she begins shouting, her voice oddly chipper.

"Come and listen to this, girls!"

Upon entering the radio room, we hear what seems to be a large group of people cheering and firing weapons into the air.

"What the hell is going on, Mila?" I ask.

"Wait, wait," she says gleefully, her entire body practically vibrating as she bounces on the spot. "They will say it again in a moment, I am sure of it!"

Sure enough, over the frequency of a still cheering crowd a voice crackles over the radio,

"...*Benito Mussolini and Claretta Petacci, his girlfriend, have been captured at the lakeside village of Dongo...*"

Well, this is turning out to be quite a month. That's one of the main dictators of this war finally captured. This of course is a major coup for the Italian partisans and I have no doubt there is going to be some partying in the Alps tonight.

"They should just shoot the fucker in the head," Petra snarls.

"I think he should be handed over to the Allies and made to pay for his crimes," Mila says, looking over at us with a smile. "It'll hopefully end in the same way, but at least the whole world will be able to play a part in it."

"Oh, shut the fuck up," Petra snaps, glaring over at Mila. "Get me a fast car and I will go down there and shoot the fucker myself."

I sigh. Petra's still angry that she wasn't able to get a chance to kill Göring herself; she hates it when she misses a target. As long as Mussolini get what is coming to him though, it doesn't make a difference to me.

After Mila lets us go, I take myself off with my sketching pad and head off into the nearby mountain trails. I need a bit of time away from any news or talk of war, and taking in the natural beauty of this country is exactly what will help me to get away from that.

I spend the rest of the day leisurely strolling through the woods and sketching whatever nature offers to me. Forest animals, landscapes or perhaps a woodland, anything that appears with each and every turn.

The next day is just like any other. It starts out with Petra and I sitting around the kitchen table as we eat breakfast and drink coffee, chatting away to those who nip in and out as the morning progresses. It feels peaceful, easy almost, as if there isn't a war raging throughout the rest of Europe. Sitting back in my chair, I watch the day go by with a smile tugging at the corners of my mouth.

It doesn't last for long, though. Not long after, Mila is yelling through the house again, her voice passing by the kitchen.

"Everyone, come quickly!" I hear her cry as I look towards the door. "Radio room. Come, come!""

I get up from my seat and trail after the others in the kitchen. We follow her chants of "Here, come here!" until we all crowd into the radio room, some of the girls spilling out of the doorway. One radio in particular is crackling with life, its sound echoing throughout the room.

The crisp radio voice

"...Mussolini and his mistress have been shot, driven overnight to the small town of Giulino di Mezzegra, near Lake Como." The crisp radio voice announces. I hold my breath; no one else makes a sound as the presenter continues. *"They were both placed in front of a stone wall and shot to death using a machine gun..."*

There is silence as the radio dies down, the news undoubtedly turning around in all our minds. Turning to look at us all one by one, Mila grins widely. Then, as if the pin finally drops, the room erupts into a symphony of cheers and claps as some of the girls crowd together, pulling each other into joyous hugs.

Everyone delights in the news, calls for celebrating erupting over the shouts. Everyone except Petra, that is.

I watch as she turns on her heels, grumbling under her breath and pushing past some of the girls. There's a buzz of excitement in the air while the girls begin to disperse. I make my move to leave as well, only Mila stops me in my tracks.

"Hannah, please stay for a moment," she says, closing the door behind the last girl. "I have some news and it isn't good."

Once we were certain all the girls have left to celebrate, Mila begins.

"This isn't something to be shared with anyone else, Hannah," she explains. I nod my understanding and she continues. "Apparently, the US forces attacked Göring's home yesterday. The information I have been provided is sketchy at best, as they never stated which residence was attacked, but there is a high chance it may have been the one we raided."

"Thanks for telling me, Mila," I reply, reaching for the door handle. "Just keep an eye out for any further information, but only share it with me." The other girls don't need the burden that can come from this, so it's for the best they don't know.

I leave the radio room and it isn't long before Mila joins me and asks if we can go on a stroll around the grounds. As we walk, she starts bringing me up to speed regarding the most recent Allied attack.

Apparently, the Royal Air Force has bombed the complex at Obersalzberg, a large complex of buildings and bunkers built for Hitler and high-ranking Nazi officers. It included the Berghof, Hitlers Bavarian retreat, though it was revealed that Hitler wasn't in residence at the time; instead, he was hiding away in his bunker in Berlin. The Air Force raid was a success of course, reducing most of the buildings to rubble, including the one we had booby trapped. What a relief.

April 30th 1945

What a day to remember. The airwaves are bursting at the seams while cheers erupt throughout the house. Hitler is dead!

The Soviets had penetrated far into Berlin city. Before they could reach Hitler though, he and Eva Braun committed suicide. It is said that their bodies were then taken outside and set on fire. Surely this can only mean the end of the war in Europe now.

Days after, every newspaper and radio station is still ablaze with the news of Hitler and Mussolini's demise. These past couple of days have been nothing but joyous for all those affected by these two dictators, and it has even been said that April 1945 will be a month to remember for years to come.

It doesn't take long after that for the Allies to achieve victory. In fact, it only takes a matter of days.

On May 8th, 1945, Germany unconditionally surrenders to the Allies, officially marking the end of a six-year battle against tyranny and dictatorship across Europe and Africa.

The whole world is celebrating this day as 'V-E Day'. We get word that street parties are erupting across almost every country, tears of relief and cheers of joy echoing throughout broken cities and country homes. Hearts are full, hope has once again been renewed and the celebrations go on for days.

Well, not every city across Europe is celebrating, of course. Some of them no longer exist, and there are those who even aided in this war that won't join in the cheer thanks to their shame.

This happiness doesn't last, and it isn't too long before anger begins to burn across mainland Europe.

Chapter Fifteen

Hannah

The war isn't over for everyone.

The battle in the Pacific is still raging. Japan are headstrong and steadfast in their determination to take over and dominate the other Asian countries.

Fighting against the Japanese has not been restricted to just the US and Australia and, as those two countries have helped us here in Europe, we are now aiding them in their struggle. Now we stand shoulder to shoulder with their fellow Allies, battling on both land and sea with no end in sight.

We have nothing to offer the Pacific theatre really due to our looks. Yes, we do have a couple of Asian ladies in our circle but they are nowhere near ready; we haven't even informed anyone of their existence either. For now, it's better for us to concentrate on our own future.

Meanwhile across Europe, the struggle to survive is not quite over for some people. It isn't long before street gangs emerge, Vigilante groups who are taking justice into their own hands and seeking out their fellow countrymen and ladies who had openly collaborated and sympathised with the Nazi's.

Nazi women are being dragged into the streets. In front of large crowds, they're stripped naked and have their heads shaved before being marked; this ensures that everyone knows who they are and what they supported. The men are being shot. In many cases it's not even once but a few times, with some even being reported to have bullets in them that reach double figures.

We are quickly coming to the end of May and it has become apparent that even Göring has survived. In fact, he actually surrendered himself to the US on the 5th May so as not to be captured by the Soviets, the coward.

It's also emerging that as a final order from Hitler, one of the high-ranking officials has sent out a *'Kill on sight'* order against Göring for high treason. Of course, this drug-fuelled Nazi isn't willing to go out by the hand of his once closest allies, nor by the hand of the Soviets. That won't stop him from getting what's coming to him, of course; we, the Soviets and his former allies simply have to bide our time before one of us inevitably strikes.

I am heading off to meet with the Major at the London HQ whilst Daphne is meeting with our American friends. This is in an attempt to ensure that they know we are here if they require our skills at any time in the future.

Daphne will also be checking in with our girls and offering them anything else they require to help them gain a solid foothold in the US. Whilst over there, she will also be dealing with our last consignment of goods, of course.

One of our major objectives is to ensure that all our legal outlets, – regardless of their function – is steadfast. Upon my return from London, Petra and I are going to Tortuga to visit our island. Once we arrive, we will establish some trusted, well-paid locals to take care of the island whilst we are not there and will also instruct them to build new rooms. It is our intention to make this island a retreat for at least thirty ladies at a time to stay on.

Daphne will join us there once she completes her tasks in the US and together, we will spend a few days getting all this sorted out and finalised.

June 1945

After our prolonged stay on the island, we return home. The two new buildings at home are now fully complete and the girls are doing an excellent job of filling each room with new a residents.

In once occupied Europe things are getting heated. Political battles between France and Britain are on-going. The de-unification of Nazi Germany is well under way. Brazil declares war on Japan whilst the Japanese Prime Minister Kantarō Suzuki states "*We will fight to the last*".

As I was outside having a smoke and playing with the dogs in the sunshine, Mila comes running out of the house and towards me.

"There's a message from London," she cries out. Gathering my things, I hurry indoors to the radio room. The message has already been decoded and reads: '*Report to HQ immediately*'. End of message.

I pack a few things and within an hour was on a plane. I can't help but be a little excited, hoping this was a mission. Once there, I was made to wait the mandatory period of an hour or so at HQ before I am ushered into the Major's office and take a seat.

He does not waste any time with the usual pleasantries.

"We have known for some time about the so called *'Ratlines'* These are escape routes for high-ranking Nazi's," he says the moment I am in the room, pacing back and forth with one hand behind his back, the other holding a freshly lit cigarette to his lips. "Here is what we do know; one runs from Germany to Spain, the other from Germany to Italy.

"Now, we are almost certain they both lead to South America. What we need you to do, is establish the actual routes and produce a list of destinations and contacts. You will pose as the wife of a high-ranking German officer. Easily established as you are German."

"Am I alone on this, or can Petra join me, Sir?" I ask. "Four sets of eyes and ears are much better than two, after all." I asked.

The Major pauses and stares at me for a moment. "Yes, that's fine," he says, but he doesn't sound pleased with the idea. "But make damn sure she understands that this is a covert mission only. That means *no killing.*"

"Okay," I nod my understanding and stand from my chair. "I have all I need. I will report back as soon as I have something concrete to report, Sir."

I hold my hand out to shake his, only for the Major to ignore me and sit back down at his desk while he begins sifting through paperwork. Without a word I turn and leave the office to head for the next available flight home.

Once home, I gather Petra and Mila and we discuss the operation in great length. Unsurprisingly, Mila has already gathered some information on this subject. Together with the file from London and the file from Mila, we come up with a solid starting point.

Something we are missing though are some crucial elements. However, Mila has been studying this for several months now and she thinks she has the answer.

Petra and I pack a bag and head off to Madrid, Spain. Once there we will make contact with one of Mila's people; she has been developing a network around the world of hotel workers. They can be a great source of information, if you use the correct stimulant. Generally, money works best.

Arriving in Madrid, we head for the Hotel Palace situated in the centre of the city. It's a very well-established hotel, dating back to 1912. After booking in we get straight to work; our contact in fact is the hotel check-in manager, who has worked here for over twenty years. He is a small, bald-headed fellow with a massive moustache, one that is so big I am sure small birds live in there. Anyway, he speaks perfect German so communication is easy.

He informs us that he has proof that over the past few weeks, several high-ranking Germans have passed through his hotel. He hands over a list of names, which we will send over to London and Mila for verification. As well as that, he tells us that some of the staff witnessed all of them entering a few of the Catholic churches close by.

"What business do the fucking Nazi's have entering Catholic churches?" Petra asks me under her breath.

Now, we are fully aware that some Nazi's follow the teachings of Christianity, but Catholicism? The Catholic church is hated as much as the Jewish religion by the Nazi party, even more so by the SS. So, the question still remains.

Later that day we receive a coded telegram from Mila.

Through her vast network, she has come up with two names: Charles Lescat, an Argentinian who was studying in France and is now a known Nazi collaborator, and Pierre Daye, a Belgian national who has also recently been identified as a Nazi collaborator. Neither of them can no longer be found.

This day has produced nothing but more questions. For now, it is time for bed and quite possibly an hour or two pondering over today's events.

Over the next few days, we send various messages to both Mila and London, firstly requesting they check the list of names from the nearby hotels against known Nazi Party members. Secondly, that they provide us with as much information they can on the names Charles Lescat and Pierre Daye.

It takes a few days but eventually we get a reply. Some fifteen or so known SS officers have passed through Madrid over the last few weeks. At least five high ranking Third Reich officers have also passed through.

It seems Madrid is some kind of central meeting point for fleeing Nazi's. We are in the right place, but we still have no idea what the Catholic church has to do with all this. Is it possible that they are simply using the churches as a meeting place?

We turn to the hotel network, asking them to provide lookouts at each of the churches; after all, there are six of them only a few minutes away from this hotel. It would take Petra and I days, if not a couple of weeks to gather intelligence on all these locations. So, if we spread some money around we will get the help we need.

If this is a central meeting area for fleeing Germans, then it isn't going to be long before someone spots a blonde haired, blue eyed, white skinned person. They will stand out in any crowded place, just as we do. One thing we have in our favour is we can at least dress like the locals and blend in a little.

With this in mind, Petra and I go shopping. Colourful, flowing dresses and patterned skirts along with single-coloured, loose-fitting tops allow us to fit in with the locals. Now, it's back to work.

Forces men have a way about them. Their walk and the way they hold themselves makes it so that even if they do change their clothing, you can still spot them. These are some of the things we ask the hotel workers to look out for.

A couple of days of sitting around in the Spanish heat and we finally get a break. One of the girls from the hotel has just spotted a middle age man entering the San Lorenzo church. Petra and I head over there as fast as we can with the girl in toe.

Once inside, the girl points out a man sitting alone about four rows back from the altar and towards the centre aisle. Taking up different positions around the church, Petra and I watch him with keen intent.

After an hour or so, we witness him get up and, as he is passing the priest, covertly hands him a booklet before exiting the church. I signal to Petra and she moves quickly to intercept the priest as he heads towards the door.

Without making it obvious, she trips and bumps into him, knocking the booklet from his hand. Reflexively, the priest reaches out to grab Petra.

"Thank you," Petra says all too sweetly. Once she has steadied herself, she bends down to pick up the booklet and hands it back to the priest before following him out of the church. I wait a few moments before taking my leave and return to the hotel.

"It's called *'The Protocols of The Elders of Zion'*," Petra explains once I enter the room. "There was also a star of David on the front."

I pause at the title of that booklet; I have heard it somewhere before, but I can't be sure where or perhaps even *when*. Shaking my head, Petra and I quickly send this information over to Mila and London and go about our day.

'The Protocols of The Elders of Zion'... I can't seem to get those words out of my head no matter how I try. I have seen that booklet somewhere before, I'm sure of it. Or perhaps I've heard the words spoken prior to this day, but where...

It isn't until Petra and I are eating dinner that I remember exactly *why* I know of that booklet.

"Shit!" I cry out, jumping from my seat while Petra begins choking on her pasta. "I know where I've seen that booklet!"

"Fuck... Fuck's sake, Hannah!" she wheezes, sputtering while she catches her breath. "What the hell is wrong with you?"

"I've got it. The booklet," I say, turning to Petra and giving her a swift whack on the back. "It was mandatory reading in all schools."

I explain to Petra that the booklet dates back to the early 1900's, first published in Russia 1905. It is mainly read to portray the Jewish community as conspirator against the state. It goes on to describe their so called 'secret plans' to rule the world through economics, the media and fostering religious conflict. It's a terrible publication that was later discredited by the London Times newspaper in the 1920's.

It's the most antisemitic book I have ever had to read. The German version is full of hatred for the Jewish community, with its text often referred to by Hitler and his followers in their speeches. It is an awful publication, one I was happy to see the back of once I left school.

This is all starting to make sense now. If this is a general meeting point for smuggling Germans out, then they would certainly use something like that as an introduction. Most people wouldn't be seen carrying that booklet, let alone in a public place; only those devoted to their cause would soil a city outside of Germany with such a publication.

However, the question still remains: Why Catholic churches and, it seems, Catholic priests? Why are they involved in these Ratlines?

"This whole thing is giving me indigestion and a big fucking headache, Hannah," Petra growls, pushing her plate of pasta away.

"Well Petra, we need to look at the other churches and try and work out how many are involved in this," I reply, placing my knife and fork on my plate of unfinished food. I've lost my appetite and I've had enough of this day, so I head off to bed.

Everything I have told Petra about the booklet is confirmed by London and, over the next few days, we hear reports of more Germans arriving in the city. We set about putting tails on all of them, day and night; they can't even use the toilet without us knowing about it, and every person they have spoken to is logged. Mila is doing an excellent job with these networks and they are proving invaluable.

A day later, Petra follows a target to another church named the Holy Christ of Faith. She times her passing perfectly; once her target takes out their booklet, she walks by just as they discreetly pass it over to the priest, and even heard the target whisper *"The protocols of the elders is the pathway to enlightenment,"* in German.

This has to be the final piece of the puzzle we have been looking for. With a copy of the booklet and the correct pass phrase, we are now ready to move forward with the rest of our plan.

We return to the hotel and change into something more up-market, but not so expensive we might be considered suspicious. Gathering our forged German papers and our copy of the booklet, we head towards one of the other four churches to find out just how many of them are involved in this plot and choose the Church of Saint Joseph.

Sitting together quietly, we take out the booklet and place it in a way that even from the altar, the priest can see it. It isn't long before he makes his way towards us as I hold out the booklet and casually repeat the code.

"The protocols of the elders is the pathway to enlightenment," I say as he takes the booklet from my hand and acknowledges the exchange.

"Return tomorrow," he says simply, making his way back to the altar.

Thanks to our surveillance of the other Germans, Petra and I knew this would happen. We just didn't know what happens next due to our targets going to the confession box. By tomorrow, though, we will know.

We return the next day and, sure enough, we are ushered into the confession box. Well, I was at least, as there is only room for one person at a time in there.

Through the confessional window, I have over our papers with two new photos and a request for our new destination, Argentina.

"We are heading for Argentina to join our husbands," I reply, making sure to dab my eyes with a handkerchief for good measure. "They are both Generals in the German Army. We just want to be by their sides once again, as you can understand."

The priest listens attentively, sifting through our papers before saying "I understand. Pease return this coming Friday." Handing the documents back, I quickly leave the confessional and make my way out of the church with Petra following close behind.

We spent our next two days acting like tourists and partake in shopping, drinking coffee and admiring the scenery around us. Finally, Friday arrives and we return to the Church of Saint Joseph where the priest leads me back to the confessional.

Once I'm sat in there, he hands me two sets of new documents which I slip into my bag. I can inspect them later. For now, though, I will simply allow the priest to believe I trust him.

"You must go to the Red Cross and apply for a 'Displaced Persons Passport'," he instructs me as the new papers rustle in my bag. "Use these new documents and this letter of recommendation." Through the confessional grate, he passes me the final piece of paper before closing the small door between us and promptly got up to leave.

I wait a few seconds before I take my own leave and head out of the church, the papers now secure in my bag.

Back in the safety of our room, we take a closer look at the documents the priest has provided us. Taking pictures of each one, we then hand the camera over to our man here and request he develop the pictures and send them straight to Mila. Our man readily agrees and sets off to complete our request.

The documents are new identity papers issued by the Vatican Refugee Organisation and stamped with the Red Cross emblem. The letter is very interesting; it is from the local Bishop recommending that we are provided with the required Displacement Persons Passport immediately.

Gathering everything we need; Petra and I make our way to the Red Cross building. It's quite large and easy to get lost in, but after asking a few of the locals we soon find the correct floor. Taking a few flights of stairs, we soon find ourselves on the *International Committee of the Red Cross* floor and enter a waiting room, there are already a few other people seated and waiting their turn, so much like them Petra and I settle in for what might be a long wait.

Petra and I spend some of that time scanning the room and trying to remember faces. It's an impossible task to remember them all but together, we might be able to match a few faces to names upon returning home. It's also a great exercise to waste time while keeping us on our toes.

After an hour or so it is our turn. We go into a room and sit at a desk, hand over all our paper work and two more pictures. The man examines them and looks up at us both once before asking if we can wait. Getting up, the man leaves us at the desk with no indication of how long Petra and I will be sitting here.

He returns around thirty minutes later, checks both of the new passports and looks us both over again before finally stamping them with the Red Cross seal.

Handing over the documents to Petra and I, he simply tells us to "Have a good trip."

Once we are back at the hotel, we repeat the process from earlier and take pictures of the documents and request that they be developed and forwarded to Mila and London. After this, we only have one more step to go: Applying for our visa.

That will be a job for tomorrow, though; all this sitting around is tiring in its own way, so Petra and I go have some dinner before heading off to bed.

We immediately head for the Argentinian Embassy the following morning and straight towards the visa application section. It looks to be another waiting game; we find a couple of seats and wait our turn.

Once we are seen to, it's a simple process overall; handover our passports to be checked, have a visa inserted before finally paying our way and it's off we go. Thankfully, this only takes us ten minutes or so, which means that all we have to do now is prepare to go home and report what we have found out so far.

Returning to the hotel for one last visit, Petra and I pack up our bags before heading downstairs to check out and thank the hotel staff for their help. Before we leave, though, we ask to speak to the manager one last time. Handing him a generous sum of money to keep both himself and his staff sweet, we bid our goodbyes to the people of Milan and make our way to the airport.

We finish off our written reports on the plane home, making note of the stages for this 'application process' to ready ourselves for our sit down with the Major. For all we care though, our mission is complete.

Although the mission itself didn't involve the act of killing any Germans, both Petra and I have found the overall experience quite intriguing. What was most surprising, of course, is the involvement of the Catholic Church and the fact they are helping a lot of wanted, high-ranking Nazi officers to escape, as well as other Nazi sympathisers.

During our journey home, we discuss the possibility of this plot going all the way to the top. Is the Vatican also complicit? Is the Pope knowingly helping Nazi's to escape? If I hadn't been a part of this mission, I don't think I would believe it myself.

Within a few hours we are in London and on our way to the SOE HQ. As we travel into the city, we can see that the process of rebuilding has already begun. There are teams of both adults and children clearing away the rubble, banding together to remove the debris and all that is a reminder of what once was. Large piles of debris have been collected and placed at one end of each street while people remove what is left of their belongings from their former homes, using whatever they can find to transport it.

Once we enter the city centre, we can see shop owners sweeping out their shop fronts and collecting any salvageable stock. Once again, we catch sight of the growing piles of wreckage, as well as the truck drivers that are making their way down the street to collect and remove it all so that new piles can form.

As I watch this scene play out from my window, I cannot help but be amazed; the British are truly resilient, ready to work together and build anew, even when everything they have known has been taken from them. Even now they stop to help others, never allowing someone else to struggle while they move the bricks and remnants of a place they once called home. It is truly inspiring.

If I had been born later than I was, I would have missed out on meeting and witnessing such people from so many different countries. Even in the grips of pending death, these people have found both inner strength and courage to continue the fight. They never give up and yes, while their courage may sometimes cost them the ultimate price, they do it with their head held high.

War is a dirty business. It changes people, even those younger in life, it's effects forever rooted deep within our minds and souls; we shall never be the same again. Our futures will forever be in turmoil now, affected by the war and the horrors it will continue to inflict upon us even years after its end.

I pull away from these thoughts when the car rolls to a stop in front of the Baker Street HQ. Leaving the car and entering the building, we are ushered straight into the Major's office. It seems he is in a hurry. Sitting behind his desk, he looks up at us both as I the door shuts behind us, echoing in the quiet of the room.

Stepping forward, I hand the Major our written report and give him a quick overview of what transpired. As I speak, the Major stands up and heads towards the cabinet that holds his bottle of scotch and pours out three generous glasses of amber liquid. Handing one to Petra first, he finally passes me one before returning to his desk. Raising his glass high, he makes a toast.

"To those we have lost, your sacrifice shall not be forgotten," he says, his voice unwavering and proud. "To those who have survived: Thank you."

We throw back our drinks before finally sitting down and place our glasses on the desk.

"Ladies," the Major says as if in greeting, inclining his head once to Petra and then me. "Exceptional work in Spain; I don't think you will need to go to Italy, now. They will most likely be using the same methods there."

Pausing for a moment, the Major looks between us both before placing his own glass down on the desk and, if I am not wrong, I think I heard him *sigh*.

"This will be your last mission with us here at the SOE," he explains slowly, his eyes softening at the admission. "The war is over now and, for some us, I believe it is time to move on."

I feel my blood run a little cooler than normal. "Are you retiring, Sir?" I manage to ask. Sitting back in his chair, the Major simply shrugs.

"Not too sure, to be honest," he admits. Lighting a cigarette, he takes a quick drag before standing to pace the room and continues. "There are major changes afoot. The SOE, I fear, will simply be no more within a few months."

I feel Petra stiffen beside me, but I dare not to look at her.

"What do you mean?" she asks.

"Rumours. Back shatter. Nothing is written in stone as of yet, but it looks like the SOE will be swallowed up by one of the 'M' sections," he informs us, sitting back down in his chair. His gaze begins to roam the office, taking everything in as though he won't see it again after this.

My stomach drops at the thought, but this is the reality of war. If it has taught us anything, it is that nothing is permanent. Not even the SOE.

Silence settles between us as the Major continues to look around the room, his eyes, usually hardened with years of training, grew softer, his brows slowly drawing inwards as the reality sinks in. Leaning forward in my chair, I slide a hand across the desk.

"It has been an honour to work with you, Sir," I say gently, my voice unusually quiet. "Thank you for believing in and trusting us."

Taking my hand in his, the Major shakes it firmly with a stiff nod.

"It has been a pleasure working with you both," he says, and I can swear I hear his voice crack at the end.

I finally look over at Petra. She's sat with her back straight, but much like the Major, her eyes tell me a different story; she's fighting back tears, her bottom lip pulled between her teeth as she shakes her head. She doesn't want to believe it, doesn't want to think about what this might mean for us.

Standing from my chair and slightly shaken legs, I look towards the Major for what might be the last time. He begins to stand as well, his hand outstretched for one final handshake. Shaking my head, I think it's time for a more fitting farewell.

"Is it fine to request a hug, Sir?" I ask. I can practically feel the heat of Petra's glare beside me; there she is. "A final gesture of not only our appreciation, but also our respect for you, Sir."

It takes a moment, but the Major slowly nods his ascent and moves from behind his desk. Arms open wide, he pulls me into his chest and holds me close. He's warm, warmer than I ever expected and surprisingly gentle yet firm as he holds me for what seems like an hour.

When I finally pull back, I realise my eyes are wet. Quickly bringing a hand up to my face, I begin rubbing away the tears as the Major and Petra manage a stiff embrace. It is oddly sweet for them both, a quick exchange that ends with Petra stepping back abruptly and the Major offering her a quick nod.

Turning to the door, I take hold of the handle and pull it open. Then, grabbing Petra by the arm before she can think to walk out, I turn back to the Major and look him in the eye.

This is the man who has continued to believe in us, someone who pushed us to our limits and watched us grow. A person who has always been there for us, a man who can only think of as family.

Smiling, I incline my head towards him one last time.

"Good luck, Sir."

Coming out 2025, their journey continues!!!